WEREWOLF MOVIE

WEREWOLF MOVIE

STEPHEN ST. FRANCIS DECKY

Frayed Edge Press
Philadelphia, PA

Copyright 2025 Stephen St. Francis Decky

Published by Frayed Edge Press in 2025

Frayed Edge Press
Philadelphia, PA 19101

http://frayededgepress.com

Cover image by Stephen St. Francis Decky
Cover design by A.R. Melnik

Library of Congress Control Number: 2025940635

Publisher's Cataloging in Publication Forthcoming

Names: Decky, Stephen St. Francis.
Title: Werewolf movie / Stephen St. Francis Decky.
Description: Philadelphia, PA : Frayed Edge Press, 2025.
Identifiers: LCCN 2025940635 | ISBN 9781642510683 (pbk.) | ISBN
    9781642510690 (EPUB) | ISBN 9781642510706 (mobi) | ISBN
    9781642510713 (audiobook)
Subjects: LCSH: Musicians -- Fiction. | Friendship -- Fiction. | Sound recording
    executives and producers – Fiction. | Werewolves -- Fiction. | New Jersey
    -- Fiction. | Philadelphia (Pa.) -- Fiction. | BISAC: FICTION / Horror /
    Psychological. | FICTION / Performing Arts / Music. | FICTION /
    Psychological.
Classification: LCC PS3604 E25 W47 2025 | DDC 813 D--dc22
LC record available at https://lccn.loc.gov/2025940635

one.

(South Jersey, 1989)

(Rick)

I'm a musician at heart so my whole life pretty much revolves around making up and playing songs, except during the day when I also work at a print shop in Collingswood, New Jersey. My boss is Mr. Henley, and he handles all of the customers as well as most of the important work. Since I'm the only other employee here most days, there is hardly ever anybody else in the shop.

"Rick, ya gotta get them orders ready to ship by four o'clock," he says to me today.

"Oh, okay, Mr. Henley."

It's just about noon. I'd like to go to lunch but I bought a bunch of records yesterday so I should probably just wait and have a big dinner when I get home. I try to eat well and I don't drink or smoke: I can't stand the smell of either. Some of the clubs my band plays in are so smoky, it can be hard to breathe at times. Plus, you need to take a shower afterwards to get the stink off. Still, there's nothing better than playing live, I guess.

I can't think about the shows right now, though—I need to focus on printing these orders that are going out today. I lied to Mr. Henley to get this job. I told him I worked for a printer in Philly which was totally not the truth. When I applied, I brought in some posters and things that I claimed to have worked on. Mr. Henley said he liked my stuff, and that's how I got the job. It's easy so I didn't really have to work hard to learn it.

❰O❱

Now it's three o'clock. Mr. Henley is still out to lunch. A woman keeps calling and leaving messages: "Call me back, Joe," and "Where you at, Joe?" It's not my job to answer the phone, so I don't.

At four I'm done. I take a few minutes to clean up and make sure everything looks alright. Mr. Henley is still not back so I grab our outgoing packages— a couple boxes of fancy business cards heading out to the city—and carry them down to the post office myself. I get kind of excited as I'm walking down Collings Avenue, because as soon as I hand this stuff over, these two jobs will be officially done. Printing can be boring and monotonous but I get a lot of ideas for songs while I'm doing it, and even if me and Mr. Henley are the only people who really care, I'm always kind of proud of the work we do.

❰O❱

When I get home Gia is there. She doesn't really live with me but she has a key to the house so we can load up her van and leave together when we have a gig. Tonight we're headlining at the Khyber in Philly.

"We're gonna kick some ass tonight," she says. "You ready for it?"

"Ha, maybe," I say.

Gia has been playing drums in bands with me for as long as I can remember, and she's always excited to play. I'm excited too, but I'm a little nervous about this show because of the two new songs we're trying out; I asked my friend Dale and his friend Frankie to sing back-up but I get the sense that Gia doesn't think that's such a great idea (and she's probably right). We won't know for sure until we give it a shot, though—it's hard to tell how anything really sounds until you go out and play it in front of people.

It took me a minute, but I just now noticed that Gia has dyed a white streak into her hair, which makes her look a little like that character from Josie and the Pussycats. I'd like to tell her this but I don't; it's mostly because I'm thinking about something else: another song. It's a new one that hasn't been written yet, but I'm the one who's gonna write it. It might take me a week to get it down, but even if it takes me five years to do it right, I'm gonna finish it. That's just how I am.

Except I usually write three or four songs a day and they only take me about an hour apiece.

❮O❯

The show goes alright except for the two songs we did with Dale and Frankie. That seemed like it would be fun but, um, it just didn't work. Gia drives back to the house with me afterward and we're both pretty beat from hauling all the equipment in so she winds up sleeping on the couch. I'm on a bed upstairs but it's more like an old cot so I don't feel guilty—when Gia isn't here, I usually sleep on the couch myself.

❮O❯

In the morning when I get to work the door is locked. I knock a few times but nobody answers. I'm not sure what to do, so I go to the corner and buy a couple of donuts. When I get back to the office, the door is still locked. I've got Mr. Henley's home number on a piece of paper in my wallet—for emergencies only—so I go to the payphone outside the donut shop and call the number. His wife answers on the second ring.

"Oh, Rick, I'm so sorry!"

She tells me it was a stroke that put him in the hospital on his way to lunch yesterday. He was lucky or smart enough to pull over while he was having it otherwise he might have caused an accident. *"…but he was always thinkin' of other people first,"* she says.

He lived, in the hospital, until eight o'clock last night.

When I hang up the phone I feel mixed-up and sad. My donuts are in a bag outside of the office but all of a sudden I don't want them anymore. But because they cost a dollar I go back and get them before heading home.

When I get there, Gia is just stepping out of the bathroom with her hair wet from taking a shower. I look at her and say, "Hey, guess what? My boss died."

"Whoa!" she says.

We talk for a minute but she has to go to work so we say goodbye. I slip into the studio to write songs but also to think, except it's hard to do either right now because—now that I'm thinking about it— doesn't this kind of mean I'm technically out of a job?

I head downstairs and look around for a newspaper so I can check the classifieds but I can't find one. I'm a little mixed-up about everything right now so I lay down on the couch to *really think* for a minute, but instead I wind up just conking out for an hour or so.

(Dale)

A lotta people think Glassboro State College is a kooky party school, but it's always seemed kinda ho-hum to me. I graduated from there last year, and I still live in a big ol' house just a couple blocks from campus. My girlfriend Carly lives with me, which is great, but there are four other people there as well, all of them recent grads who haven't figured out what the heck to do yet.

I'm driving to my friend Frankie's right now but first I stop to buy a soda and some candy bars. I'm hungry so the candy bars taste pretty good.

There's a lotta traffic on the road, which makes me think: *There musta been a car crash.* I'm not in a real hurry, since Frankie's prob'ly sleeping and if I'm late it will just mean he's got extra time to rest. He's sleepin' now because he had to work late at the movie theater we both work at and was recording with his friend Eric after.

When the cars start to move again, they move real slow. Eventually, you can see police lights and then a pair of smashed-up cars on the side of the road. There's an ambulance coming, too. From where I'm at I can see a man in green clothes talking to somebody with a bloody shirt. All of a sudden I hear a siren and when I look in the rear-view mirror I see another ambulance coming, along with more police cars. *Jeez, that accident musta been bad,* I think, and for the rest of the ride I make sure to drive extra careful.

《○》

Frankie's been livin' with his grandmom since he was in high school, mostly 'cuz she needs a lotta help. He could be living with his mom but she married some guy a few years ago who turned out to be kind of a jerk; they decided to move up north and told Frankie he could come with them or stay with his grandmom and he was like: *I'm stayin' with Granny.* He told me they don't even call him on Christmas or his birthday. Sheesh.

Anyway, Frankie is an usher at the movie theater but he also does the marquee signs on the side of the building and at the end of the parking lot. That means he's the one who climbs up on a ladder and spells out the names of the movies that are playing—along with their showtimes—with big plastic letters on lit-up signs that are almost forty feet high. He does this a couple times a week, when new movies start and also when the screening times change for the weekdays. Because he's not supposed to do this until after the last show of the day has started, he has a key to the theater, and because he has the key, on some nights he and Eric—who is the one who holds the ladder while Frankie climbs up and changes the letters—sometimes bring guitars and drums into the theater after it's closed and record music. They do this because they love making up songs but also because the theaters have really great acoustics, so even if the songs are terrible, they still kinda *sound* really cool.

Because it's sorta dangerous doing the marquee signs, Frankie gets paid a lot more money for doing that than he does for being an usher. I should know—I'm the Assistant Manager at the theater, and I make out the payroll every week.

☾O☽

When I get to the house, Frankie's grandmom says, "He's asleep," and won't let me in. She closes the door so I have to knock again.

"Hi—Frankie said to wake him up," I tell her. "We're goin' to a show."

"He didn't tell me anything about a show," she says, and I think: *Get outta my way, Granny.* "He has to work tonight."

"No, he doesn't," I say.

She stares at me through the screen door for a minute and then she unlocks the latch and opens it.

"Be nice," she says.

"Oh, for sure."

I step inside. The house smells like soup and mothballs. There's a TV on but everything else is dark: All the windows are closed up with dark curtains and there's no lights. I know where Frankie's room is so I walk down the little hallway, and because there's no door to his room, I knock on the wall beside his bed.

"Telegram for Frankie," I say.

"Mmmph," he groans, then opens his eyes. "Just gimme a sec to brush my teeth."

"I'll wait outside."

"Okay."

Frankie's grandmom watches me walk back through the living room. I look over at the chair she's sitting on and notice that she's staring at me. I don't know if I should say goodbye or not, so I just wave instead, then walk back out to the car, telling myself: *She's pretty scary for a scared old lady.*

☾O☽

We're actually going to two shows tonight—one is at Nick's on 2nd Street, but that's not 'til around eleven. Before that, we're going to the Khyber because the Rick Bowen Band is playing and since I'm friends with Rick he asked if me and Frankie could sing the back-up parts for a couple of new songs. "The parts are pretty easy," he'd said. "We'll practice them in the sound check. Then when we're doin' the show, you and Frankie'll run up on stage and sing them with me."

Wow, that's gonna be fun, I thought, and now in the car on the Ben Franklin Bridge with Frankie next to me, I still think it's gonna be great.

(Frankie)

I sleep with headphones on and the radio playing so I don't have to listen to Granny talking to herself. Most of the stations around here are terrible but I can get WPRB from Princeton sometimes and also the college stations from Philly. I had to do a report about the radio in high school so I know it was invented in another country, and the first thing that got sent through it was Morse code. The place it was sent to was Newfoundland, and the guy who did it was named Marconi. That was in 1901.

In 1906, Reginald Ferrender did something: he sent his voice and the sound of a violin over the airwaves. People kept fuckin' with the radio and eventually, around 1920, they came up with the idea of amplitude modulation, which I don't understand but when it's shortened it's AM.

Later, somebody figured out frequency modulation: FM. But before that there were record players and later there were tape players, then eight-tracks and CDs, and so on. There must be a thousand ways to listen to music and I like them all. Plus, anything's better than listening to Granny being creepy and weird.

(O)

This house is gross. It's small and it smells funny and it's cold in the winter 'cuz Granny won't turn the heat up—she'd rather shiver under a pile of blankets on the couch.

The truth is, Granny's totally bonkers. When she's not talking to herself and yelling at people who ain't here, she's sitting in a chair in fronta the TV, holding a book. I know what book it is—it's called *Delicate Remembrance*, a romance novel. I've checked Granny's bookmark a couple times in the past month and a half; it's always on page seventy-nine, which means she's been starin' at this page for at least six weeks straight.

She won't eat anything but oatmeal and bananas and butterscotch candies. She won't leave the house. Sometimes she hollers at me for things I didn't do. "You used up all the towels," she told me last week. "There's seventeen towels in the hamper and I can't fit anything else in it."

"Granny, I didn't use seventeen towels. I didn't use any towels at all."

"Then how'd they get in the hamper?"

You put 'em there! is what I wanted to say. *Who the hell knows why, but you put 'em there and now you don't remember it!*

There's no point in arguing with her or being mean about it. If I moved all her stuff out onto the back porch and made her live out there she prob'ly wouldn't even notice, and that's the sad part. She has a couple other grandkids and a daughter—my Aunt Annette, who was my Dad's sister—but none of them ever stop by and they hardly ever even call. I take her to the doctor when she's got appointments and I pick up her prescriptions but I'm pretty sure what she's got ain't ever gonna get any better. It's confusing because even though I get really annoyed with her sometimes I still completely love her—she's my grandmom, ya know? Also, no matter how lame she might seem she's the only person I know who offered me a place to live when I didn't have anywhere else on this planet to go.

☾O☽

As soon as I leave the house, though, Granny's like totally the last thing on my mind. Especially tonight—I'm singing back-up with

Dale for the Rick Bowen Band and I'm pretty nervous about it. In the car on the way over to Philly, Dale plays a tape Rick made of the songs we're supposed to sing.

"Alls we gotta say is, '*I'm drivin' awaaaaaaaayyyyy to-night*,'" Dale sings. "Then we just say, '*Doo-doo-doo-doo-doo-doo-doo-doo*,' all the way to the enda the song."

"What about the other one?"

"The other song? We just say, '*La-li-la, la-li-la*,', every time it comes to the chorus."

"Chorus?"

"This part." He reaches over and turns the volume up on the stereo. This song kinda stinks, but I can do the "*La-li-la*" part, no problem. Dale rewinds the tape and we practice both songs again and then all of a sudden we're there, in Philly, looking for a place to park the car.

❰O❱

You might think that putting up the marquee letters at the theater would be scary, since the ladders are kinda rickety and I'm well over thirty feet in the air some nights with no ropes or anything to secure me. I've never been afraid of heights, though, and even if I'm also a little clumsy—which, now that I think of it, is not a great combo—I get a kind of thrill when I'm up there that I can't get anywhere else in my life: it feels dangerous because it is dangerous but the view is amazing and I also get paid for it.

So I might not be scared of heights, but there's one thing that definitely terrifies me: *being on stage*. This becomes really obvious during the sound check at the Khyber. There's hardly anybody here for that and I still feel like I'm gonna barf when it's my turn to sing. It's even worse when the show's almost over and Rick is waving for me and Dale to come up on stage. My stomach is turning once we're up there and I can't even look at the crowd without getting dizzy. When I actually start singing, it sounds like somebody's punching me in the throat.

The second song we do feels even worse but when it's done the show's over and I get a huge feeling of relief. Dale shakes my hand and then we help Rick and Gia pack up their stuff.

"Oh jeez," Dale says to me as we're carrying the drums out to the van. "We forgot all about the show at Nick's."

"Damn," I say. That show was supposed to start at eleven and it's already five after. The band that's playing there is called Space Drunks—they're like totally my favorite local hardcore band and Kebby the singer is my idol.

We say goodbye to Rick and Gia then run down the street to Nick's. The doorman doesn't charge us anything because he knows Dale from somewhere and when we get upstairs the music is so loud and screechy my head starts splitting right away. But it's awesome to hear some of my favorite Space Drunks songs live, especially *"I Got a Message for You and You're Not Gonna Like It,"* and *"Get Outta My House Before I Kill You All."*

When the show's over Dale drives me home and we congratulate each other for doing a good job at Rick's show, even though in my head I know we were terrible and Rick would have to be out of his mind to ask us to sing with him again.

two.

(Rick)

It's too nice out to stay inside all day so I go to Philly instead and buy some records. I should be looking for a job, I guess, so I buy a newspaper, too, which I read on the Speedline on the way home. I'm just getting to the classified section when the train pulls into the Collingswood station.

As soon as I'm back in the house I make some cereal. While I'm eating I get an idea for a song, which makes me think the best thing for me to do right now would be to start writing some new music. Upstairs, I have a whole recording studio, with drums and everything, so I can record pretty much whenever I want.

If I could, I'd do nothing but make up songs all day. I know a lot of people who make music really love being on stage and playing for an audience, but that can be a hassle too—you have to carry the equipment, which is heavy, and you gotta remember all the notes and the words you're supposed to sing. Crowds can get mean, too, and sometimes we do bad shows. But at home, when there's nobody else around, I walk up the steps to the studio and it feels like the whole world is super-small; everything I need from it is right there in that little room, and I only really ever feel complete when the red RECORDING light is flashing.

((O))

Later on I come downstairs and see there's a message on the machine. It's from Gia.

She says, "Rick, hey. I was gonna come over but I wanted to get dinner, too. You want me to bring somethin'?"

I call her back.

"I was thinkin' maybe I'd get a pizza?" she says.

"Nice," I say, and Gia says she'll pick it up before she comes over if I call and order it first. I'm in the middle of recording a song but it's six o'clock and the only thing I ate all day was that bowl of cereal. So I call the pizza place and tell them what we want.

"Five minutes," they say. I tell them that someone named Gia will be picking it up, and that she's tall with long red hair.

"Doesn't matter. Five minutes."

Alright. I head upstairs to shut the studio down and then I straighten up the kitchen a little. By the time Gia gets here I'm starving, so we sit down and eat right away.

"I gotta practice with Jenn and Tina tonight," she says. Jenn and Tina play with Gia in a band called Crank Tops. Gia also plays drums in another band with me and two other people; that band's called Devilbaby, and we're pretty popular in Philly right now. But *right now* doesn't really mean much, I've learned that.

Before Gia leaves there is this minute where we're both standing by the door saying goodbye over and over again. But it's almost like we're saying something else—I'm not sure what it is and I don't think Gia does either, so neither of us actually comes out and says exactly what we're thinking.

But no matter how good it is to see her and how hard it is to watch her leave, I'm glad she's gone. It means I got the rest of the night to play.

((O))

On Sunday, Dale and Frankie stop by around six o'clock.

"We're goin' to see the new werewolf movie," Dale says. "You wanna come?"

"I can't, I'm recording," I tell them. I finished six new songs since yesterday, and two of them are decent. "Plus, I'm supposed to practice with my band tonight."

"Oh, okay," Dale says. "Frankie's got a new tape."

"Yeah, here," Frankie says. He hands me a cassette in a plastic case. On the cover is a piece of bread with a face; it's saying something to a cowboy, and in the background the sky's purple with little yellow stars.

"Awesome," I say, and I'm smiling because Frankie's band is pretty neat—they record everything on old tape recorders so the quality's always *really* bad. But they've got this crazy energy and the words are super catchy and sometimes totally hilarious. "When's this from?"

"Like two weeks ago," he tells me. "Me and Eric drove down the shore one night and made songs in the car on the way. You can hear the engine hummin' the whole time."

"Nice!"

They leave and I sit down to drink some juice and listen to the tape.

(Frankie)

I'm wiped-out from working so much but the werewolf movie makes me feel better. The part where the werewolf bites a guy's arms off is gross and awesome, and I get a little teary-eyed at the end when he's crying and saying, "Sorry guys, turns out I'm a werewolf after all"— even though he's not a werewolf anymore 'cuz they shot him like a hundred times and he's dying.

Me and Dale go to the diner in Runnemede afterward and I finish two cups of coffee before I realize Eric's sitting at a table in the back with a couple kids I knew from high school. I wave to him and he comes over to sit with us.

"Hey Frankie, hey Dale," he says. "Whaddya up to?"

"We just saw the new werewolf movie," Dale tells him.

"It was fuckin' dumb but I loved it," I say.

The waiter brings more coffee and the hamburger Dale ordered, then Eric tells us, "There's nobody home at my house—my Mom went up to see my brother in Maine. Actually, I tried to call you earlier to see if you wanted to play."

"Yeah, I'd love to!"

"How 'bout you, Dale?"

Dale swallows a big mouthful of hamburger then shrugs. "I gotta get to work early tomorrow," he says. "I been late every day this week."

I'm secretly glad to hear this because although it's fun playing with Dale, it kinda holds me and Eric back a little bit. He's got a great voice but he likes to make up his own words, and I'm not sayin' mine are better, but all Dale ever sings about is girls and stuff. Plus, all the best songs me and Eric ever did were ones we did with nobody else around. It's just better that way.

I drink one more cuppa coffee while Dale finishes his burger and Eric says goodbye to his friends. Outside, we say goodbye to Dale then climb into Eric's car.

"Whaddya say we switch around tonight?" I say. "I'll play guitar and you play drums."

"Uh, that never works," he replies.

This is sorta true because I can't really play guitar to save my life. But if you plug the guitar through a distortion pedal and crank the amp all the way up, it's so noisy you can't tell what the hell I'm playing anyway.

"Tell ya what," I say. "We'll do two with me playin' guitar first and then we'll switch."

"Alright, that's cool."

Twenty minutes later, the amp is cranked to ten and I'm standing in front of it with this wall of staticky noise blowing up in my face. It hurts like hell but if I scream back at it while I'm playing I feel like I'm at least as powerful as the sound, which is a pretty good feeling.

(Dale)

When I get home Carly's still awake.

"I'm hungry," she says. "Let's make some pancakes."

I just had that burger at the diner but did I eat anything else today? Sheesh, I can't remember for a sec, but then outta nowhere it hits me: *I had eggs for breakfast.* They weren't so great, but now, even though I just ate like an hour ago, the thought of having pancakes seems like a great idea.

Everybody else who lives at the house—Rebecca, Joey, Rich, and Amanda—is asleep so we have to be quiet. Carly does most of the work, and she's only wearing underwear and a t-shirt. We start kissing and one set of pancakes gets burnt. But then we get serious about the pancakes and in the end, we wind up making almost twenty.

They taste so good I can't stop eating them. I've been doing this too much lately—I mean, eatin' all this junk at the enda the day. It's prob'ly why I've been feeling so gross and have had so much trouble sleeping lately. Right now, though, these pancakes are *definitely* hitting the spot.

After washing the dishes, we go upstairs and lay down but I can't sleep—I'm too worried about not getting up on time tomorrow and my stomach's in knots. To make it even worse, Carly is snoring super loud.

I get up to use the bathroom, but then instead of going back to the room I head downstairs and conk out on the couch. But I keep waking up every couple minutes to check the clock. By the time the sun is up, I'm like totally exhausted. But now it's too bright to sleep in here, so I go down into the basement and look for something to sleep on. I find some pillows and some parts from an old couch we used to have, which should work. I pile everything up and then I lay down, like a giant rat. It's nice and dark and quiet down here so I fall sound asleep like right away.

When I wake up it's after noon and I'm like three hours late for work.

(Frankie)

My head's buzzing from all the feedback and noise and I don't feel like sleeping so I get Eric to drop me off at the diner on Route 41 for breakfast after we get done recording. Although I do the marquee two or three nights a week, being an usher is still my main job at the theater. I gotta be in at 11:30 this morning, which is still three hours away, but I inhaled so much caffeine in the past twelve hours it feels like my whole body is humming.

It's a five-minute walk to the theater and I got a key to the front door so I go inside and wash myself up in the Men's Room. There's a kid who cleans the theaters at night and I see him carrying trash out toward the back door when I come out. When he leaves, the place is empty, so I lay down on one of the couches in the lobby and conk out for an hour or so.

Around 11:15, the morning shift people start showin' up. Dale's not here yet (even though I remember him sayin' he had to be here early) and although I'm not supposed to do this, I start lettin' everybody in. At 11:45, there's still no sign of Dale, so I call his house.

"What's up?" It's Carly, Dale's girlfriend, who I sort of know but not really. I ask her if Dale's coming to work but she says he's not there and she doesn't know where he's at.

"Oh, okay," I say and hang up.

When Sully the projectionist comes in, he looks mad. "Who let everybody in?" he asks, because only the projectionists and the managers are really allowed to open up in the daytime. I lie and tell him I had to fix some letters that fell off the marquee and he doesn't question it.

"Dale's not here yet, though; I don't know where he is."

"I'll tell ya where he's gonna be if Ms. Leo finds out," Sully says. "He's gonna be over at the unemployment office." He stomps upstairs looking pissed 'cuz now he's gotta get the cash-drawers on toppa setting up the day's movies. I try to help out but he doesn't say thanks or anything—he only just barks commands.

It's almost one o'clock when Dale finally shows up. The first shows for today were really slow so we didn't have any problems, which was kinda lucky. But Sully's old and grumpy so I let Dale—who has brought along a dozen donuts—know about it right off the bat.

"Sully, shmully," Dale says, waving his hand. "I can handle him, no problem."

An hour later, I go up to the office and find Dale and Sully sitting at the desk, playing cards with the box of donuts between them. Dale gives me a wink so I figure he's got it all worked out.

three.

(Rick)

I start looking for a job on Monday but it's hard because I really don't want one. The bills are paid for this month and I've got enough money in the bank to pay them for two more months if I don't eat too much and don't buy too many records (except this afternoon while looking for places to fill out applications, I passed Final Vinyl Records in Westmont and stopped in just to look but wound up finding some things I really needed to get). Plus, when I get back there's a call from J.C. Dobbs in Philly: They want me to come and do a show tomorrow night since the band they had lined up got into a car crash on the way up from D.C.

I decide this show will be an acoustic one, just Rick Bowen and his guitar—I'll tell Gia and everybody that they asked me to do it like that, which they kind of did (after I mentioned the idea) so it's not really a lie. Plus, I've got all these new songs and I'd really like to try them out on my own.

Usually I never think about the money we get for a show—it's never much, believe me—but that money might really help right now. How much could I make for real if I book as many shows as possible? I could do one or two solo shows a week, and maybe host an Open

Mic? I'm also thinking maybe it'd be good to do a show with Bee Plasm (that's Frankie's band), since they've never played live before and I think the crowds in Philly will really dig them. The tape Frankie just gave me is called *Snappy Apple Pap-Gun* and it's even better than the other two I got from him, *Amateur Slap-Rat* and *Dorothy's Bowl of Cats*.

While I'm listening to the records I just bought, I start making phone calls. I line up three shows with two calls—a pair at 13th Street Pub and another at the Pontiac Grille. Then I ring Dale and ask if he thinks Bee Plasm might open for the Rick Bowen Band later this month.

"I'm not sure," Dale says. "I don't think they really know what they're playin' mosta the time so it might be kinda like an experiment." Dale has recorded with Bee Plasm before; what they do, he told me, is line up a boom-box-type tape-recorder, count to four, then start. Frankie usually has notebooks with words to sing but they get other people to sing sometimes too. "I'll def'nitely ask him but he's pretty shy—he almost left the bar the other day when it was time for us to come up and sing with you."

"Oh, yeah, right," I say, recalling the sight of him, ghost-faced and shaky on the stage beside me. "I just think it'd be great to play with them. It might be a mess but it could be fun too."

"Lemme give 'im a call and I'll call you back."

"Thanks, Dale."

I hang up then debate calling Gia and asking her to go get something to eat with me. The problem is it's always great to talk with her, but when we're together I don't get anything done. Sometimes I wish we could record something together, just her and me, but it always seems like we need a third or fourth person there to really write something good. We've been playing in bands together and have been friends for ten years but we've never written a song that was just her and me together. Why is that?

☾O☽

While I'm wondering whether or not I should call her, the phone rings and it's Gia—she wants to know if I feel like getting something to eat and mentions maybe going to see a late showing of the new werewolf movie. Because I'd really like to focus on other stuff, I tell her I'm not sure about the movie but maybe we can go get something to eat in a bit.

"Did'ja find a job?" she asks.

"No, I think I stopped looking."

"Can you swing it for a while? I mean, without a job?"

"I don't know. Maybe?"

"It'll all work out, Rick, you know it. Catch ya in a bit!"

"Okay."

Dale calls back almost right after I hang up and says, "Hey Rick, I think they'll do it. Frankie said him and Eric and some other people they play with are gonna do their first show at the movie theater this Saturday night, around midnight."

"What? You mean, at the theater you manage?"

"Yeah, when all the movies are over for the night. I don't think they're planning to do a real concert, they're just gonna make up new songs on the spot."

This sounds insane. "Wait, so it's their first show but it's not a *real show*? Who's gonna be there?"

"Just people who work at the movie theater and their friends, I guess."

I'm not actually hearing an invitation but I'd *really* like to go.

"Anyway," Dale says, "Frankie said they can definitely open for you. Do you already have a date lined up?"

I take a look at the little notebook I use to write down notes and ideas for shows and see that we'll be doing at least three gigs a week—between the Rick Bowen Band and Devilbaby—starting next week. "Let's say three weeks from now," I tell him. "A Friday night. I'll talk to the guy at the Khyber and tell him these guys are new and kinda cool."

"Nice."

Dale hangs up and I start getting ready to go out, feeling sort of hopeful in a funny kind of way.

(Frankie)

When I get home from work the first thing I see is Granny sprawled out and motionless in the middle of the living room floor. It's gotta be the most unsettling thing I ever seen, and for a second I almost walk right back out the door. Instead, I take a deep breath and move a little closer. Her eyes and mouth are open but you can tell she's not breathing or seeing anything.

I take another deep breath, this time noticing the rotten smell in the air.

It's pretty gross.

I get this rush of panic as I walk to the kitchen, thinking I gotta call the police or an ambulance. But instead of calling anybody I sit down at the table and stare at the wall while squeezing my fists together to keep from freaking out.

She's dead. Granny's dead. How can that be?

For a couple minutes I can't even move, but I know eventually I'm gonna have to call somebody. But who? Aunt Annette, the police? I get the sense that nobody's gonna feel all that bad about this even though Granny was a great person who would help anybody out any way she could, at least until she got sick. After that, people just stopped visiting, and she only got worse when Gramps died and left her with nothing to do and nobody to hang out with.

I feel this real heavy wave of sadness, but I can't cry 'cuz at the same time I'm also realizing something else: I'm gonna get kicked outta this house. It's not mine and I'm sure it'll have to be sold or somethin', right? Where the hell am I gonna go then?

I go into the living room to get a better look at exactly what I'm dealing with here but I can only stand it for a couple seconds before I start feeling nauseous and head back to the kitchen.

The phone rings.

It's Dale. He says Rick Bowen wants Bee Plasm to play with him somewhere in Philly, like a live show. The idea of playing live has always turned me off because I don't really like practicing and I also got that stage-fright thing. But a chance to play with Rick Bowen—

who is pretty popular in Philly, I've never gone to a show of his that wasn't packed—is just too big to turn down.

"Okay, yeah," I say. "I'll have to ask Eric, but I bet he'll be psyched." I tell Dale about the show we're planning to do at the theater this Saturday, and how we're thinking it will be like sometimes you're in the crowd watching and sometimes you're up on stage playing.

"That sounds awesome. Am I playin' too?"

"Yeah, for sure."

"Cool!" he says, then adds: "Whaddya doin' tonight?"

"Ahm…" I open up the back door to let some fresh air in. "I gotta clean this place up a little. My grandmom… she kinda freaked out."

"Yikes. Okay, see ya tomorrow then."

"Yeah," I say, and as I'm hanging up the phone I get this idea that's sorta scary and maybe impossible but also probably very dumb. There's a pen in my hand and I got a notebook in fronta me but I'm not writing anything—I'm thinking about this scary idea, and the more I think about it, the less scary it seems and the more sense it starts to make, no matter how dumb it might sound.

And then, just like that, I know exactly what to do next.

《O》

It's later now and I'm driving down Route 41 toward the abandoned Kindley Landfill with Granny in the backseat. I could go to jail for this, I know it, but it's already too late and there's no turning back. The reek of the landfill keeps getting heavier and stronger, but I don't mind it at all—anything's better than the pervasive stink coming up from the backseat.

I got no problem facing the facts here: I'm dumping Granny's body. I loved her, she helped me out, she was there when my dad died and she let me stay at the house when my mom and stepdad turned out to be jerks. In a way it's a good thing she died now because eventually somebody woulda showed up and made her go to an old-people's home, which woulda wiped out what was left of her already scrambled brains and I guess her bank account too. At least she died at home, on her own terms.

There's a fence that opens with a tap from the front bumper of my piece-of-shit '74 Chevy. I've known this landfill all my life, it's part of the scenery in this part of town. I only have a couple of vivid memories of my Dad, but one of them was when I was like five years old: I was in the passenger seat of his car as we passed this place and I yelled, "Daddy, look—it's a mountain! Can't we get out and climb it?"

"You don't wanna climb that mountain," he'd said, which is the kind of solid advice I've been missing since he died.

But I'm halfway up that same mountain right now, dragging Granny across some murky pulp and into the landfill's stinking depths. The sky's all cloudy and rumbling in the distance but from where I'm at, with huge mounds of trash looming up in all directions, I can't help feeling totally enthralled by the strangeness of being here. If you could close up your nostrils, it might seem like some exotic mountain range, or part of another planet.

But it's the stink that keeps reminding me of where I am: I'm gagging and coughing all over myself while trying to keep a grip on Granny's sad, lifeless shape. Her glasses are hanging from one earlobe now and her nightdress—along with my shoes and pants—are like totally slicked over with this oily-red stuff that's so heavy and sticky and wet it feels like it's alive.

Eventually I find something that looks like a lake. Fuck knows what it's made outta but I'm guessing it's some kinda chemical sludge mixed with acid-rain and mud. I'm on the verge of puking so I pull Granny up to her feet and push her in without even hesitating. She goes down face-first, floats for a few seconds then sinks so fast the lake actually gulps.

By the time I get back to the car it's raining and I'm shivering and my body's hurting all over. I open up the windows to get the smell out but as I make my way back to Route 41 I start feeling sick; I pull over and slide out but nothing happens. When I look up, I see a van coming toward me and just as it's about to pass the driver honks twice, which almost gives me a heart attack. The van doesn't stop though so I hop back into the car and speed out toward home.

Inside the house, I get the urge to call somebody but it's late now and besides there's no way I'd ever be able to explain what I just did. The best thing to do is just forget about it: it's probably impossible but after washing my hands for half an hour then making a cheese sandwich and eating it out on the back porch, I start thinking it might not be as hard as it sounds.

(Gia)

Most people I know don't wanna practice every day but I like to feel confident on stage, so guess what? I don't mind practicing at all! I'm working with three bands right now and I try to play with at least one of them every day. In fact, this afternoon I spent a couple hours with Ray from our band Devilbaby then later drove all the way out to Pitman to work on some new stuff with Jenn and Tina from my other band, Crank Tops. In between I had dinner with Rick and even though we didn't play, pretty much alls we talked about was what the setlist's gonna be for the show we got comin' up. Rick's band is definitely the easiest one I play with 'cuz he writes all the songs and they never get too complicated. Devilbaby doesn't always feel all that original but the live shows are loud and crazy and a total blast.

I feel the best playing with Jenn and Tina though 'cuz it really feels like we're working on something big; it's a lotta fun but we're super serious about it too. I think the best way to describe it is like this: we have a good sound that could potentially be great, and if we keep working at it there's a chance that people will really start to notice. That might be the best you can ever hope for in any band, but I feel like our chances are pretty damn good.

Anyway it's getting late and starting to rain a little and Jenn lives all the way out near Glassboro State College, where she teaches. It's a hike to my place in Haddon Heights so I bolt as soon as we finish up.

I don't come out here all that often but every time I do I seem to get lost. Why is that? Is it 'cuz the roads out here are haunted, like the Bermuda Triangle? Ha, maybe!

I do my best to be careful this time but still I somehow wind up making a wrong turn and the next thing ya know, I'm driving down some dinky road and this rank smell comes up outta nowhere. Yuck! It's gotta be a landfill or something so I close the windows and try to wave the stink away from my face.

There's only one other car on the road in fronta me and it's swerving a little so I slow down to make sure I don't whack it. Eventually the car pulls over and I see this kid get out and walk over to the side of the road, all hunched-over like he's gonna yak. He looks a little like that kid Frankie who's always hangin' around our shows—the one who sang with us the other night—but it's hard to tell 'cuz of the rain and mist and everything. Plus is he even old enough to drive? I give a couple quick honks as I'm passing just in case but when I look in the rearview mirror the kid's either disappeared or climbed back into the car.

The whole scene kinda gives me the creeps so I punch the gas and haul ass 'til I hit Delsea Drive and make a left toward 42, psyched to get home and catch some well-earned z's.

four.

(Dale)

It's like Tuesday or Wednesday and I'm late again, but this time it's bad because it's the phone that wakes me up and Ms. Leo is yelling at me so loud and so fast that I can't even hear what she's saying. When she's done, she hangs up, and I'm left starin' at the receiver with the alarm clock beside me still going off, except instead of saying 9 a.m. like I set it for, it says 11:50 a.m., which means I'm only really like a half-hour late...or did I just get fired? I don't really know for sure so I get dressed as quick as I can and start driving to work.

When I get there the first person I see is Frankie.

"She's really mad, huh?" I say.

"We could hear 'er yellin' all the way down here," Frankie replies. "I tried callin' you at like ten to see if you wanted to get breakfast but nobody answered."

"I think I got a problem," I tell him. "I mean, I can't wake up no matter what."

"Maybe you just need a bigger alarm clock."

"Maybe."

I go up to the office and Ms. Leo is there.

"Goddammit Dale, you *gotta* get here on time!" Ms. Leo is a short, giant-haired woman who will not take any shit from anybody. She's not actually supposed to be working today so she's wearing a pair of sweatpants and a loose sweater instead of her usual fancy sport coat and pants. The casual clothes make her look like a big elf. "I'm not gonna tell you anymore, and you know I mean it. This is the *very last time.*"

"I'm sorry."

"You're gonna be sorry if you're late tomorrow, I guarantee it."

So that's how today starts but after a while Ms. Leo leaves and I have the office to myself. There's not much to do and it's not busy, so I volunteer to run out to get pizza for the staff. After I pick it up, I'm tempted to drive the extra five or ten minutes out to Full Circle Records in Blackwood, but then I remind myself that I've got that pizza in the backseat and it would be kind of a jerk move to keep everybody waiting for their lunch.

Frankie comes up to the office around four and I notice he doesn't look so good.

"You think I can leave early?" he asks. "It's been slow and I ain't feelin' so hot."

"Ya sick?"

"Nah, I just couldn't sleep last night and I gotta do the marquee later."

"Any shows tonight?" I ask.

"Ah, I don't think so—I'm not gonna be able to do anything except sleep, I think."

"Okay, yeah, go get some rest."

Frankie leaves and eventually Roger the night manager for tonight shows up. He tells me Ms. Leo called him today and said she'd scared the pants off me, except Roger calls her "Mr. Leo" and makes a joke about her weight, which isn't really funny because you hear shit like that all the time about her and after a while you wanna ask, *You got the guts to say that to her face?* She's the boss for a reason and she's good at what she does. Plus, she didn't fire me so right now I'm thinking Ms. Leo's pretty much the nicest person on Earth.

In any event, I still feel shaken when I leave, rememberin' that voice on the phone, the useless alarm clock, and my big ol' tired ass crawling out of bed en route to a job I wasn't sure I even had or wanted anymore.

(Rick)

I'm sitting in the kitchen eating a piece of pie when all of a sudden I get this great idea: I'm gonna mix down some new songs and make a limited-edition tape out of it. The last time I released an album was like a year and a half ago, and I've recorded close to a hundred songs since then. Usually I'd wait to get the money together and have a record pressed, but selling a legitimately exclusive tape at shows won't cost much to produce, right? Plus I feel like fans really dig that kind of thing.

As I'm thinking of this, I get another idea—a bigger one: If I'm gonna start releasing my own tapes, why don't I start my own label? I know some pretty awesome bands—including my own—and it would be like cutting out the middleman to get their music out into the world.

Would it be worth it? Would it be *possible?*

I mean, Philly is a great place to play but it's not as big as it might seem when you're in it. The Rick Bowen Band got voted one of the Top Ten Best Bands in the city last year but when you think about it, up until last week I was still working thirty-five hours a week at a job I didn't care much about and I'd still be working there now if my boss didn't die. If a record label's gonna work, it's gonna need a bigger reach.

There's a knock on the door that I'm thinking is probably Gia, but when I get up I see a big shadow looming through the glass so I know it's not her. Instead, it's Dale Bursmith.

"Rick, hey."

"Dale, how's it going?"

"I'm alright, I was just passin' by." Dale is wearing a white shirt and a tie so I know he just got done work. "I almost got fired today."

"Hey, maybe you can join the club."

"You got fired?"

"No, my boss died last week. I thought I told you."

"No, jeez, that sucks. You alright?"

"Yeah, I just don't have a job."

We're both a little hungry so I make us some toast with butter and jelly. Dale talks about going out later and I tell him I got songs to work on. I also yawn a few times, feigning fatigue, when in truth my mind's swirling with ideas on how to get a record label off the ground.

"Well, I'll see you at the Devilbaby show Thursday," he says, finally.

"Yeah, I'm super-psyched about that," I say.

The last minute that Dale's here feels really long, but the second the door closes and he's gone I sigh with relief because I think best when I'm alone and right now *I've got some serious thinking to do.*

(Frankie)

I'm still at Granny's house although every sound I hear is completely freakin' me out. You can say you don't believe in ghosts but when you're alone in a house where somebody just died there's something in the air that's hard to explain, even if it's just your own head getting used to the absence of the person who just died's presence. I'm scared about the cops, too, and Aunt Annette or anybody showing up out of the blue or even calling. I don't know what the hell I'd say to any of them and I need this house right now, there's nowhere else for me to go.

Goddamn, what the hell did I do? I dumped a perfectly-explainable dead body in a lake of toxic grossness at the landfill. Why?? I guess I could say I temporarily lost my mind with grief but I'm pretty sure that's not true. Also, there's just something downright nasty about dumping bodies wherever you feel like it.

As much as I'd like to sleep somewhere else, I'm also scared to leave. Even worse, I'm exhausted—I was up all last night and I've got to do the marquee tonight. But I feel weird sleeping on the couch because Granny died in that room and the bedroom feels even creepier right now.

One thing that helps, though? Opening up the curtains and the windows. The rooms here look totally different as soon as what's left of the sunlight hits them, since Granny—and Gramps, when he was still here—preferred to keep the place as dark as possible, with nothing more than the light of the TV to brighten the place up.

《O》

It takes a while but eventually I conk out in the bedroom. I try not to think about what might be under the bed but as I'm drifting off the thought that something good might be hidden somewhere in this room takes the place of the thought that something bad is waiting to attack me.

I forgot to leave the hallway light on so when I hear something crash in the kitchen I wake up to complete darkness. It's nighttime now and I bonk my head on the windowsill climbing out of bed. It's quiet for a second but then I hear another weird sound from the kitchen, followed by what feels like something moving through the hallway, going right past my door. I find the light switch and flick it on.

The first thing I see when I look into the kitchen is that the freezer door is open. Even though I'm watching as this happens, I jump when a piece of ice falls down through the door and explodes on the floor. *I musta left it open*, I tell myself. *I was exhausted, right?*

After turning on the light in the hallway and then all the lamps in the living room, I go back to the freezer and close the door. The clock on the wall says 9:30, which means I have to meet Eric at the theater in like half an hour.

"Granny?" I say out loud, but just saying her name freaks me out so I put water on for coffee then go into the bathroom to wash my face and brush my teeth.

I'm alright. I slept. Everything's okay.

I drink the coffee and have a cheese sandwich but it's the last of the cheese so I have to remember to buy some when I'm done with the marquee. I'm gonna need coffee too, I notice, and as I'm getting ready to make another cup, my eyes get all watery just thinking about the house and how it's gonna be completely empty when I leave for work.

(Rick)

I practice with Devilbaby in Ray the lead singer's basement on Tuesday and then there's a show at Nick's on Wednesday and another one at Dobbs' on Thursday. The Wednesday gig is packed and we make more money than we ever did at one show, which is cool. The Thursday show is alright too, but while we're in the middle of the set I see a guy in the crowd that I noticed last night too—he's not wearing a suit but he's dressed nice and you can tell he's from somewhere, a record company probably, the way he's staring up at us all like he's analyzing everything.

After the show, he walks up to the stage as we're packing up our stuff.

"Rick?" he says.

"Yeah, hey."

"Donnie Ifrinn, O.L.C. Records." He shakes my hand and I get this funny feeling that I can't quite place: it's like either something totally awesome's about to happen or I'm in danger; I can't tell which. Maybe it's both?

The guy smiles. The stage lights are making his eyes look orangey-red. "Any chance you might wanna go get a coffee with me when you're done here?" he asks. "Something to eat maybe?"

"I am kinda hungry," I say.

"Whenever you're ready."

I give him a nod and he walks over toward the bar. Gia asks me who he is and I tell her; her eyes open wide but I say, "This might not mean anything," which is totally true. Still, it feels good to have a label interested in my stuff, and besides, I'm pretty much always hungry after a show.

Donnie has a nice red car and he drives us all the way down Broad Street to Oregon Avenue, then up to Third Street where the Oregon Queen Diner is. I eat pancakes and drink a glass of milk but Donnie just orders coffee, which he doesn't even touch.

"You've been on our radar for a while," is what he says.

"Oh yeah?"

"Yeah, just following your trajectory and all—I mean, the Rick Bowen Band shows, not the Devilbaby ones. Don't get me wrong, you put on a good show tonight but it's obvious—whoever you're playin' with—that you're the talent."

I shrug because even if this is supposed to be a compliment it sounds lame. I mean, I was playing with my friends tonight. Also, even though the guys around here don't like to admit it, it's pretty obvious that the most talented musician around here is Gia, who can play any instrument and gets along with everybody.

"The thing is," Donnie continues, "you got a singular talent for *songwriting*, and the potential to put together an album of great significance. I'm not fuckin' around—I'm ready to sign you on right here, right now. To be fair, I can't really make it official in this diner, but I can give you a pretty good idea of what a contract would look like."

"Shoot."

He gives me the run-down and it sounds good—too good. It'll be a lotta money, way more than I could ever hope to make with my own label. He's pretty specific about this idea of recording one great album, though, and the plan after its release seems a little hazy. But he knows my songs pretty well, and tells me that "Pretty Decent" and "Wind-Up Car" could both be singles.

"Think about 'Wind-Up Car' a second," he says. "Go and listen to one of the bigger stations 'round here for a while then listen to that song—you'll see right away how it not only fits in but is a hundred times more relatable than the stuff they're playing."

"Uh-huh," I say, a little mixed-up again because it sounds like he's telling me that my music is ordinary enough to fit in with the junk you hear on the type of radio station I totally can't stand. The thing is, the way he puts it, he's absolutely right. I don't know how I didn't realize this before—I always thought I was doing something totally different. But when I think about what he's saying, I can see how "Wind-Up Car" really is just, like, a pop song, Top 40, a single you can tap your feet to and sing along with.

But is that what I wanna be known for?

It's been a long day and I'm tired after the pancakes, so Donnie says he'll drive me home. Something doesn't feel a hundred percent right when we get back to the car but I can't tell what it is exactly. I'm thinking about how good it'll be to tell Gia the news but at the same time it feels like there's something buzzing inside my head, or maybe around it? I'm having trouble hearing, too—it's almost like somebody's wrapping gauze over my face or tying a bag down over it.

My eyes are opened but somehow I keep missing parts of the way home, and eventually it feels like we're lost, and I have no idea where we are.

"I live…that-a-way," I say at some point, pointing my finger out through the opened window beside me. Donnie says something I can't hear because my ears are all blocked up and the next thing I know there is a forest or maybe just a garden and I'm sliding—softly—onto the grass face-first. There are people or animals moving all around me but it's too dark to see what they are or what they're doing.

I try calling for Donnie again but then somebody or something picks me up and hoists me into the air so high I can see the trees and the streets and everything else below. I get the sense that I'm either floating or flying but I can barely feel anything since I'm literally paralyzed with fear. I'm still awake enough to notice one thing: there's an animal—or what looks like an animal, a really big one with red eyes—hovering to my right and staring hard at my face. And while he's staring into my face I'm staring sideways into his and thinking, *this has to be a dream,* which it might be, except when I wake up later

I'm on the floor of my living room with the front door wide open and my head spinning as my hand reaches to my stomach 'cuz my shirt's ripped open and it feels funny there and when I pull the hand up to see what's going on I can see it's like totally dripping with blood.

35

five.

(Frankie)

The Bee Plasm show at the movie theater this Saturday is totally my idea, and it's not as random as it might sound. For one, it'll keep me out of Granny's house for an entire night, which will be a total relief in itself. Also, if I can be totally honest here, I'm still freaked-out (and embarrassed, I guess) by how scared I felt on stage last week. I'm not sure how to even explain this, but once I got up there, I felt so completely separated from my own thoughts that it seemed like I could actually see myself from the crowd. Does that even make sense? I'm not used to being that scared so what I'm thinking is maybe the best way to get over that particular fear is to just confront it. If Bee Plasm is ever gonna go out and do shows on our own, I'm gonna have to get used to the crowds, so I'm hoping this gig at the theater will be a good start.

Anyway, it's Thursday now and I'm way up near the top rung of the ladder on the marquee at the end of the parking lot. There are six screens inside the theater, and at least one movie changes every week (though usually it's more like two or three). This week, the action-thriller *You're Gonna Pay For That* and the comedy *Rat Friends III* are leaving and will be replaced on two screens by one of those terrible

Summer Kids Movies—this one's about a bear who can talk and ride a motorcycle and the title's so long it's gonna take an extra thirty minutes to spell it out on the signs.

Still, I really love the view from the top of the ladder: it's South Jersey so it's all flat below, but some nights there's a glow on the horizon that looks almost heavenly. The sky's clear and the moon's almost full so it's a little extra-bright tonight. I can see something moving through the sky too—it's not quite high enough to be an airplane but it's still moving pretty fast. From my angle, it looks almost like a car except blurry and with some thing or things either hanging from it or hovering around it. The sight of it sends a funny chill down my spine, which for a second makes me feel like I might lose my balance. I'm holding a giant plastic M in my left hand, which probably isn't helping, so I try to focus for a second and snap it into place on the marquee.

"You okay up there?" Eric hollers up from the ground.

"Yeah, for sure," I reply.

I shake my head and look back up. Whatever it was I'd seen up there a second ago, it's completely gone now.

((O))

It's Saturday now, just after midnight, and we're at the theater for the first ever live Bee Plasm show. Eric is here and so are Andie and Joey—they both play with us sometimes—as well as pretty much everybody who works at the theater and their friends. Dale Bursmith shows up later with Rick Bowen, which is sort of an honor because Rick's almost like a celebrity.

The theme of the show is *Anybody Can Be in Bee Plasm*, which means we're pulling people out of the audience to play drums, guitar, or whatever, even if they don't know how to play. This makes everything kinda sloppy for the most part but we get Rick Bowen to play bass on a couple and those songs come out pretty cool. I'm a little mixed-up about Rick because Dale and everybody else thinks he's great and he's really nice to me, but I don't really always like his music (it's a kind of goofy type of pop that always seems to be about girls or cars).

Me and Eric record constantly, so we've got like 500 songs in our repertoire. But because we never practice, we don't know how to play any of 'em. I think the songs are great, but at the same time it's pretty obvious that nobody could ever really like us for real—the recording quality is terrible, we can't sing, it's a total mess. Still, it's the only thing I do with other people that really and truly makes me happy, and I can tell by the way people are lining up to scream into the microphone here that our first show's a pretty big success.

Afterward me and Eric and Rick and Dale go to the diner. I found forty dollars in the grass under the marquee sign the other night so I treat myself to a big plate of waffles and tell everybody to get what they want 'cuz it's all gonna be on me. Rick Bowen looks a little loopy but I don't say anything about it right away.

Later, though, Dale says, "Hey, Rick, Gia said you went out with some record-company guy after the show on Thursday."

"Oh, yeah," he says.

"What happened?"

Rick hesitates with his toast, smiles and makes a weird face. "Tell you the truth, I don't know. We got into an accident, I think."

This sounds kinda kooky so I don't say anything but when I look at Eric he's got this half-grin on his face, and I can tell we're both thinking the same thing: *Huh?*

"You, uh… you still think you want Bee Plasm to open for you sometime this month?" Dale asks, deftly changing the subject.

"Oh yeah, for sure," Rick says, and that's it.

I drive Eric back to the theater to pick up his car when we're done. The sun's up so I figure it must be like 6:00, 6:30 in the morning.

"You workin' today?" Eric asks.

"Yeah, but I'm done at 5:00," I say.

"Maybe we oughta make some songs."

"Yeah. We can listen to the tapes, too," I say, because I recorded everything we did tonight on a boom-box and I'm like dyin' to hear it. "You think you really wanna open for Rick Bowen?"

"I don't know. It's like, an opportunity, I guess? He seemed like he was into it."

"He seemed like he just got back from palookaville," I reply. "Dale says he don't do drugs, though. Maybe he bumped his head or somethin'?"

"I don't know, maybe."

"Yeah. Hey, I'll come over when you're done work."

"Cool."

We crack knuckles and say *Bee Plasm* like it's this all-powerful thing and then I'm in my car driving home and alls I can think about is how great the whole night was.

(Dale)

I've been avoidin' the subject of what's wrong with Rick all night, but after we leave the diner I start tryin' to get him to talk. Gia told me something today that was pretty strange but neither of us could figure out what it really was—it's like, something happened to Rick; he either got hurt or he got signed onto a record label but nobody knows for sure.

"So," I say as we hit the White Horse Pike on the way back to Collingswood, "you think it's a good idea, signin' onto a label?"

"I don't know," Rick replies. He burps a little and we both laugh and then he says: "I was thinking of starting my own label. Actually, I was working on it all last week—I went to the county clerk's office and all and paid them for a business license. Plus, I was doing a mix for a new Rick Bowen Band cassette—like a limited-edition tape to sell at shows, the way Gia and her band do it."

"Wow," I say, because this is the best thing I've heard yet—even better than being injured/signed-onto-a-label by some mysterious record label exec. "You gonna put out stuff by other bands, too?"

"Yeah, that's the whole point—I'll get Ray to give me the tapes of all the Devilbaby songs and Gia to give me the Crank Tops stuff so I can, you know, get records pressed and distributed."

It gets quiet for a minute, but then I say, "Hey Rick, what the heck happened with that record label guy anyway?"

He shrugs his shoulders like he did at the diner but I notice his hand goes down to his side, feeling around his ribs. "We, uh… went to the diner, I guess. We talked about contracts and things, nothing definite."

"Gia said you got into a, uh… a car accident?"

"I don't know."

"You mean like you don't remember… or what?"

"Huh?"

"You don't remember bein' in a car crash?"

"No. I don't. Man, I just don't remember." He shakes his head slowly and rubs his eyes. "I woke up on the floor with like a big… like a, uh, a chunka skin taken outta my side."

"Does it hurt?"

"It's… kind of starting to, yeah. But it hasn't really 'til now."

It all sounds really weird but I'm not sure what else to say, so I let it go even though I feel like Rick might need some help. It's kinda sad to see him like this because he's a real straight-up guy and you can usually count on him to be pretty level-headed.

It's almost 7:00 a.m. when I drop him off at his house, but I'm not tired at all. What I feel like doing is playing, or maybe listening to the tapes Frankie made of the show tonight. I think about asking Rick if he might want to go up into his studio and make a couple songs but he lets out a big yawn as soon as I stop the car and says, "Thanks Dale, this was a pretty good night," and I'm all of a sudden so proud to be friends with such a locally famous and good guy that I can't do anything except say, "Take care a yourself, Rick," and drive away smiling from ear to ear.

six.

(Rick)

This week's been a little rough. I was feeling alright after playing with Frankie and Dale at the movie theater, but then my side started hurting pretty bad the next day and I decided to go to the hospital. They put some stuff on my stomach and gave me a prescription but I kept feeling like people were looking at me suspiciously there, like maybe I did something terrible.

Did I?

I honestly just don't remember.

It's a few days later now and I'm still trying to get used to these painkillers—they really zap your energy. But if I don't take one every few hours my side feels like it's splitting open and I have to lay down. It feels a little like I'm losing track of the days too; I truly almost forgot we had a show Monday night but maybe that's understandable since I've got so much stuff booked for the rest of this month.

❨O❩

Well, I'm pretty sure it's Wednesday now and the phone is ringing.

"Rick, how are you?" It's Gia; it's always good to hear Gia. "Are you comin' to the Crank Tops show tonight?"

"Man, I'd *really* like to but… I don't know, I'm still not feeling a hundred percent."

"You takin' the medicine?"

"Yeah, yeah."

It gets quiet on the line and all of a sudden I just feel so lucky to know Gia—she's totally gonna be famous and she's always looking out for me. She is without a doubt the best friend I ever had.

"Gia, listen," I say, "I'm sorry I've been acting so weird lately—"

"Rick, c'mon, don't be sorry. You got hurt and it's gonna take time to get over it." She pauses for a second and in that second I reach my hand out like I'm gonna touch her hair but alls I wind up doing is getting my arm tangled up in the phone wire. "If ya want," she continues, "I can stop by after the show to see if you need anything."

"Yeah, wow, that'd be great," I say.

I try taking a nap after I get off the phone but I'm feeling too bad about missing the show. Gia and Jenn and Tina are so fun to watch on stage, it would really take a lot for me to miss one of their shows. Plus I need them to get a demo together for my record label, which I'm still thinking I might be able to pull off, as soon as I start feeling a little better.

Eventually it gets to me and I put on a jacket and get ready to leave. Except when I open the door, I see this total darkness outside and even though I'm admitting I'm scared now I still don't know what it is I'm scared of.

Or do I?

Donnie was his name. An agent, the guy from O.L.C. Records.

I'm way late for the show by the time I finally leave the house—as it is, I'm gonna miss the opening band. I think about calling up Dale to see if he wants to go. Maybe he could pick me up from the station? I know I sound paranoid, but I'm exhausted and also nervous about making that long walk from 13th and Locust down to the Pontiac, where I think (yikes, I hope) the show is.

I call from a payphone at the Speedline, but there's no answer at Dale's. On a whim, I look into my wallet for Frankie's number, which for some reason I thought I had. But apparently I don't.

I'm not even gonna think about walking back to the house now so I buy a ticket and go up the stairs just as a train's pulling in. This is sort of a good sign, and I hop on feeling a little better, until I look over at the seat across from me and see a well-dressed guy with slicked-back hair taking a seat.

Donnie.

He smiles and loosens up his leather jacket.

"Hey Rick," he says. "Going to the show?"

"Um… yeah."

"Thought I saw you walking to the station." He reaches over to shake my hand: it feels cold, like a pile of, I don't know, ice cream? I shake it anyway then pull my hand back as calmly as I can.

"You, uh, think about what we talked about last week?" he asks

"The… contract?"

"Well, no, the ramifications of maybe signing a contract, yeah. What *might be* in a contract."

It's hard but I manage to look away for a second, just long enough to close my eyes and look back to make sure Donnie is really there. He is. This second sight of him makes the hair on my neck curl up.

"I guess… I guess I'm not sure yet," I manage to say. "I've been working on getting a label of my own together."

"That's right, you mentioned that," he says, and for the first time I notice how smooth his skin is, the dark hair pulled back tight from his forehead into a skinny ponytail, the veins that pop and roll across his neck as he speaks. "That's an idea, Rick, it's something to consider. I'd be interested in, you know, being part of a deal like that. I mean if you needed help, some financing maybe."

"I'm not sure," I say.

"Well… we should talk about it."

He nods and shrugs a little then leans back and opens up a copy of the *City Paper* I didn't notice he was holding. I'm sort of wishing

I'd had the foresight to pick up a copy of my own. As it is, I'm too nervous to close my eyes and sleep and since there's nothing to read the only thing I can do is stare out the window while the train speeds into the city.

We both get up before the train stops at 13th and Locust. I position myself so that I'm behind Donnie all the way up the steps, taking my time at the turnstile even though he's already stopped in his tracks and is waiting for me by the second stairway, the one leading up to the street. We go up together and start walking toward South Street, but even as I'm wondering how I might be able to get away from this guy, my thoughts and my vision start getting fuzzy.

I have no memory of how we get there but suddenly the door to the Pontiac opens up in front of me and Donnie is handing the doorman some money. There are like ten or fifteen people waving at me in the crowd right away; it's like everybody knows me and I know everybody, but I'm terrified because even though he was right there beside me like a second ago, Donnie has suddenly vanished.

I wave to Gia, who is up on stage setting up, and then I circle around the entire club but I just don't see him anywhere.

My eyes dart over toward the door, and I tell myself: *Go. Get outta here.* But as soon as I take a step forward, I feel a hand on my shoulder and I hear Donnie's voice whisper in my ear.

"Fuck this dump," is what he says, and just like that everything turns to white.

(Gia)

Let me set this straight: Crank Tops is *the real deal,* and we are gonna be a big-ass hit. Me and Tina and Jenn were all playing with other bands when we met, and one night after a show we were talkin' and we realized we were all total geeks for that early 60s garage band sound—ya know, that stripped-down, fuzzy pre-punk noise with scratchy vocals and bare-bones drum-kits. It's why we started playing together. We don't get much coverage yet but if you come to any of our shows, it will be wall-to-wall people and everybody knows the words to at least one of our songs. We're friends with almost every band in Philly but we're makin' some waves in New York and D.C. too, and I'm hopin' we can get our shit together and hit the west coast for a tour sometime next year.

I'm not gonna harangue anybody about not givin' us respect. I got a degree from Berklee and Jenn teaches Music Theory at a darn good school. Tina owns the record shop I manage and makes enough money to pay for a lotta the little extras we need, like duping the cassettes we put out (and sell out of) every couple months. We don't have a record deal right now but it's mostly 'cuz we're still kinda new and our sound is still evolving. We're gonna get there though, 'cuz we're in it for the long haul. Ten years from now, twenty years from now, 99.9% of the bands we're opening for now will be gone—long gone. But me? I'm still gonna be here.

Ya got that?

《O》

We're getting ready to do a soundcheck when I spot Rick in the crowd and give him a wink. Rick's helped me and a lotta people out and I feel pretty lucky to know him. Every opportunity he gets he turns into an opportunity for me too, like with shows and playin' with other bands and all. He definitely freaked me out a little last week with that weirdo record exec guy, though, and I don't wanna stay at his house 'til I know exactly what's goin' on. But he's pretty much my best friend and I'd do anything I can to help him—as long as it doesn't get *too* weird or scary, I guess.

(Dale)

Well, I guess today is the day I find out that Carly's cheatin' on me. The whole day's been kinda messed up, actually: I woke up early so I could have a regular breakfast for once before going to work but when I got to work, I found out I'm not working today—Ms. Leo changed the schedule; I remember her even telling me about it last week but somehow I just forgot. Sheesh. I went to the record store instead then stopped at Frankie's but nobody was there, not even his grandmom, so I decided to drive back home and listen to all the records I'd bought.

You know how sometimes you can tell something's wrong before you even walk in the door? I got that feeling as soon as I parked the car. I remember even looking up at the window of my room and thinking: Carly? I don't know why, just: *Carly?*

They weren't in my room, though, they were right there on the living room couch—Carly and some hairy guy I never seen before. Carly was wearing like a nightdress but still, it's hard to say *Well at least she was dressed* and feel okay about it.

Anyway, in a situation like this you never really know what you're gonna do. But because I had to pee I went straight upstairs to the bathroom and locked myself in there. My heart was thumping across my chest but once I peed and looked at myself in the mirror for half a minute, I felt like it was time to do something; I don't know what. By the time I got back downstairs, though, Carly and her friend were totally gone.

So what did I do? I went back upstairs and slept for ten hours straight.

❮O❯

Now it's later and I'm awake again but I'm still tired. There's a Crank Tops show tonight but I don't think I have the energy to go, which sucks because I figure Rick might be there and I've been worried about him. But now I'm worried about myself too; I feel like crap and everything seems like a big lie all of a sudden. Remember when Carly said Jay—my friend, I mean my ex-friend Jay—was hitting on her last year? That sounds like bullshit to me now, because I can remember times when I went to the bar or the student cafeteria and saw them sitting together, which—at the time—always seemed okay because they were both my friends and after all, it was me that introduced them in the first place. But the story sounds fake to me now, like it's missing some parts, and even though I just like snagged her messing around with *this* big jerk, the thing I really want to ask Carly about is Jay—like, *Tell me the truth, Carly: Were you messin' around with Jay too?*

It's kinda chilly in the house and I can hear Rebecca and some other people talkin' downstairs. I'm in no mood to talk but I really wanna cuppa hot chocolate, so I go down there and just sorta wave with a big fat smile when I pass everybody. When I get to the kitchen, Rebecca is there pouring a beer into a glass.

"What'cha lookin' for, Dale?" she asks.

"Hot chocolate."

"Oh, Dale, I'm so sorry—I meant to pick up more when I was at the store. I drank the last one this morning."

I close the cabinets and turn the heat off the stove without saying anything. But when I look up and see Rebecca looking at me, I know I'm about to start bawling, and when it comes out it's awful—I'm too big and goofy-lookin' for crying, I get all hunched-up with my hands running through my hair and I snort and sob like a baby. Rebecca puts a hand on my arm and asks "Holy shit Dale, what's wrong?" but I don't say anything since I'm only feeling sorry for myself because my girlfriend's a liar and I hate my job and I'm tired of living in South Jersey with a degree I don't feel like doing anything with and nothing at all in my future, so I just wave my hand then walk back up to my room and lay there feeling like shit for I don't know how long.

(Frankie)

I thought I might see Dale at the Crank Tops show but either he forgot about it or he's sleeping (which he seems to do a lot of). Either way, I stick around 'til they finish, then offer to help Gia pack up her drums.

"Did you see Rick?" she asks.

"Ahh, I thought I did," I say, thinking about it. "I waved to him but I don't think he saw me." I say this only because of the fact that Rick didn't wave back, which seemed strange since he's usually pretty friendly.

"Hmmm," Gia says. "I thought I saw him, too."

We ask around and find out that a lotta people *thought* they'd seen him but the consensus on one thing is clear: he's not around anymore.

(O)

This next part seems like it happens all of a sudden but I guess it really started when I was in high school. It has to do with a girl named Ali I used to be friends with because we had like three or four classes together and had known each other since like fifth grade.

I don't like girls. I mean, I don't hate them—I don't hate anybody. But I'm not attracted to girls the way mosta the kids I grew up with were. I'm not really attracted to guys either—well, mosta the time— but that's another story altogether. Parta the problem, I think, is my Dad died right around the time the idea of liking girls or guys started to seem like a big deal to the other kids around me, but I was too depressed to be interested in anything. Nothing's really changed much since then although I keep sorta thinking it will.

Anyway, I'm pretty naturally awkward around everybody, but when I was in school, Ali was the one person I felt most normal around. We hung out a lot, but by the time we finished eleventh grade things had really changed. My mom and my stepdad were gone and I was at Granny's sometimes and at other times I just slept in my car. Even though I usually got good grades before then, my senior year was really rough, and I only just barely passed.

After we graduated Ali went to college in Massachusetts and I went nowhere. I mean, I thought I'd be travelling all over the world after high school but instead I was still workin' at the movie theater five minutes from where I grew up. I had Ali's number but every time I got the urge to call her, I'd look at myself and feel like a nobody. *Just leave her alone,* I'd think.

But now it's a couple years later and this is the night I see Ali for the first time since graduation. I don't have to do the signs tonight so after I finish helping Gia haul her drums, I stop at a diner in Blackwood to get some coffee and write some words in my notebook. I'm sitting at a booth maybe five minutes later with a cup of coffee in fronta me when I hear somebody say *"Frankie?"* and before I even look up, I know who it is.

"Ali!" I say. She's holding an order-pad in one hand and she's dressed like a waitress. Her hair's shorter but her eyes are still green and when I look at her, I feel like she knows everything about me—there's no way I could ever lie to her, and I remember that sense of wanting to tell her everything the minute I see her.

"You look great," she says, leaning in to hug me. "Weird as usual—but great."

I laugh and ask, "What are you doin' here? Did'ja finish school?"

"Ha, no—next year. I'm just back for the summer, makin' some money here. You got a couple minutes? I'll take a break and sit with you."

"Oh, yeah, for sure."

She holds up her index finger then walks away, smiling. When I sit down I realize I'm smiling too, but I'm also nervous: I won't lie to her, I know that, but I'm not sure I can tell the truth about *everything* right now, either.

❰O❱

"Jeez, I didn't know what happened to you," she says, sitting across from me now. "I can't believe you're still around here. I thought you woulda left by now—you used to say you wanted to go to Scotland, or France? Which was it?"

I wanted to go everywhere, actually, mostly 'cuz I wanted to learn languages—even in my terrible senior year I still got As in French. Thinking about it now bums me out a little and reminds me of how much effort it's taken to simply survive the past few years. I don't get paid much at the theater and it's hard enough just scraping together the money for food and stuff. There's barely enough left over to travel back and forth to Philly, let alone Scotland or France.

"I live near Woodbury now," is what I ultimately tell her.

"I went to Scotland in the spring," she says. "Actually, I was in London and Wales too—I'll have to show you the pictures."

"Ha, yeah, for sure," I say.

When she asks me what I been doing I tell her about playing with Eric and the show we might do with Rick but then for some reason, this random story about Granny "disappearing" comes outta my mouth, which scares me 'cuz parts of it are true but most of it's not.

Ali gives me a funny look.

"Don'tcha think you should call the cops or somethin'?"

"Yeah, I'm gonna. Tomorrow." I hesitate before adding: "I'm scared to tell anybody 'cuz I'm pretty sure she's not gonna come back."

"You don't know that," she tells me, but actually I do—Granny is definitely not coming back.

We talk about getting together sometime but even as she's giving me her number at school, I'm sure it's not really gonna happen. Still, it feels like it was really important to see her right now 'cuz things have changed so much since she went away. Ali is gonna do great—everybody knows it. She's smart and her family loves her and her future has all kinda possibilities. I never had anything like that, but it doesn't mean I'm a loser: it just means it might take me a little longer to get where I belong—unless somehow I get a lucky break somewhere. But you can't count on luck, I know that.

seven

(Gia)

Okay, something's definitely not right. I swear I saw Rick at the show and it seems like everybody else saw him, too. But where the heck's he at? It's almost three o'clock in the morning and I'm sitting on his front steps just thinking the worst—like maybe he got kidnapped, or maybe he went and got hurt again somewhere? We've been friends for a decade and he's never flaked like this on me before.

It gets chilly after a while so I climb back into the van and sit behind the wheel for a minute. I wanna help him out but at the same time I feel like something bad's goin' down. Should I really even be here right now?

I oughta call the cops is what I oughta do, I tell myself.

I close my eyes for just a second and maybe it's because it's late and I'm kinda beat but outta nowhere I hear and feel this *swoooosh* of air going by overhead, as if something huge just flew by. For a minute, I'm thinking: *That was a dream, right?*

Maybe, except the van feels like it's rocking back and forth a little. Is it? My hands are all of a sudden gripping the wheel, and I'm looking out toward Rick's front lawn when I hear another long *swoooosh* passing overhead. This definitely shakes the van and also completely freaks me out because I'm absolutely wide awake right now. I reach down for the key, ready to turn on the ignition and bolt, but at the same time I can't tear my eyes away from the lawn—it's still dark out but it's late enough that you can see some light coming up on the horizon, which is a total relief except I also notice something moving across the grass. It only takes me a second to realize it's Rick.

"Hey, look out!" I holler, because I feel like there's something else out there too—I don't know what, just *something.* Rick keeps moving, kinda like hobbling toward the house. By the time I get out of the van he's at the front steps, leaning against the door and going through his pocket for a key.

That's when I feel it, and hear it: something big going by overhead once more—not like airplane-big but like animal-big. It's moving so fast that by the time I look up it's already gone. When I look back to Rick his eyes are rolling into the back of his head so I drag him into the house and slam the door shut. As soon as I let him go, he just sorta crumples up into a ball on the floor.

I don't know what else to do so I grab a blanket from the couch and cover him up, then sit down on the carpet across from him. After a minute I get up and grab a big black umbrella from a rack by the door. I take a seat on the couch and grip the umbrella tight, ready to smack whatever the hell is out there over the noggin with it.

But a few minutes later the air outside seems to settle and the sound of birds and cars starts to fill the air. Even so, I don't close my eyes 'til the sun is up all the way and the darkness is completely gone.

(Dale)

Man, I feel like shit.

The damage is done and there's nothin' I can do about it: Carly cheated on me and doesn't care. At some point during my ten-hour stretch of sleep yesterday, she managed to sneak into her room and cart out most of her clothes and records, some of which were actually mine. I should be mad, but why bother? The damage is done and that's that.

It's a long night and I'm not tired but I do manage to fall asleep just around the time the sun's coming up. I set two alarm clocks right next to my head because I gotta be at work by eleven, which is gonna totally suck, but maybe if it's slow I'll just sneak into one of the movies and tell whoever's working to grab me if they need any help.

But at the theater there's nothing I want to see and it's so slow I've got nothing to do. After sitting up in the office for like two hours, thinkin' about Carly and what a jerk she is, I walk down to the end of the parking lot and buy a newspaper out of a box. Back in the office, I call the deli to deliver my lunch and then eat it while going through the classified ads. But there's nowhere I really wanna work, nothing I really wanna do.

"Darn," I say, tossing the paper aside and going downstairs, where Frankie is jousting with Eric, using brooms for swords.

"One a you guys wanna go home?" I ask.

"Me," Frankie says. "I was out wicked late after Gia's show last night."

"You think you can handle this alone?" I ask Eric.

"There's twelve people in the building, counting employees," Eric says.

"Okay, go ahead," I say to Frankie, who jumps up and down for a second before tearing off his usher's jacket and tossing it across the lobby. I walk with him back up to the office so he can punch out.

"Dale, what's up?" he asks. "You sick or somethin'?"

"I came home yesterday and found Carly makin' out with some big hairy guy on the couch."

"What?"

I shrug my shoulders. "I'm just feelin' sorry for myself."

"Dale, that's horrible… and gross. You wanna go find the guy and punch 'im out?"

"Naw, I'm not really mad," I say, which is a total lie—the truth is I keep getting more and more pissed every time I think about it. "It's just a bummer, ya know? I mean I been friends with her for almost five years."

"That long?"

"Uh-huh."

"Dale, I'm so sorry. I'd totally get together with you later, but—"

"Naw, it's cool. I don't think I'm up for anything anyway. I might drive down the shore a little later; I think it'd do me some good."

"Well, gimme a call if ya want, I'll prob'ly be up late."

"Okay."

He puts his arms on my shoulders then jumps on me like a big cat, which makes me laugh but as soon as he leaves it doesn't seem funny anymore so I just sit back down behind the desk and think: *Man, I feel like shit.*

(Rick)

Things are definitely not going so well.

Gia is trying to help, I know, but it's starting to feel like she really shouldn't be here. I know I'm not being particularly nice to her either, which makes me feel even worse. I also keep getting this strange, persistent urge to bite the side of her head, but in a friendly, joking kind of way that I'm absolutely sure would not go over well right now.

I mention that it might be a good idea for her to take off and she's gone in a flash.

Watching the door close and listening to the van drive away should feel profoundly sad, but the level of disconnect between what's going on in my life and what's going on in my mind appears to be getting wider by the minute. I can't keep track of what I'm even supposed to be feeling.

Eventually I drag myself up to the bathroom and climb into the shower. The cut on my side is still there, but there are new ones all over me now, too. The hot water stings like hell, and I can see the blood from all the new cuts turning the water pink. Even my hair feels like it's bleeding.

My mind flips back to last night, to seeing Donnie on the Speedline then somehow losing him at the bar. But then the bar disappeared too, and from what I recall, it turned into a movie theater—or maybe I just went to a movie theater to see… I don't know, some really violent film about two people in an apartment? They're sleeping and something comes in through their window and literally starts shredding them apart with its teeth and claws? But then there's something else in the room and you get this really awful close-up of it ripping open another person's stomach and shoving its face into it? And it's all like super-realistic and the screams are horrific but after a minute there's a knock on the door and this muffled voice yells *"Pizza!"* so the two things—whatever they are—jump through the window and sorta float out across the Delaware River?

It occurs to me I should go get a newspaper and see if there's a movie playing in the city that's got a plot like that, but then I remember something else: it's the view of my house from somewhere above the trees, the lawn getting closer and then my feet landing, like in a dream that you wake up in the middle of to find yourself right there in the spot you were dreaming about.

The phone rings as soon as I'm dressed and coming down the stairs.

"Hey, Rick."

"Donnie," I mutter into the receiver, while staring at my arm and hand: the scratches and cuts are still a little bloody, and it looks almost like I just dived into some underbrush or dropped through the windshield of a car. "Donnie… I-I'm not feeling so good."

"No?"

"No," I reply, weakly. "I… I think I got… like some kinda cold."

"Man, that sounds awful," Donnie tells me. "How 'bout I come over and bring you some chicken soup? Best thing for a cold, nice hot bowl of chicken soup."

"Yeah, yeah," I say. "Donnie, I can't talk, I got a gig tomorrow—"

"Cancel it. Listen, let me tell you why I'm calling."

I pause for a second; the house goes completely silent.

"What is it?" I ask

"It's about… well, I guess it's about this cold you got," Donnie says.

"Oh, yeah?"

"Yeah. I think I might be able to help you with it. Maybe if I come by in a little bit, me and you can talk about it and figure out how to get to the root of this… this cold."

"You think it's bad?" I gulp. "Like, do you think I'm dying?"

He laughs. "Hey Rick? When did you turn into such a drama queen? No, you're not dying, alright?" He pauses then adds: "You are changing a little though."

"I am?"

"Yeah… well, sort of. It's mostly temporary, but even so it can take a while to get used to."

I kind of know what he's talking about, but not really.

"What am I changing into?" I ask.

"I don't know, man, a donkey? How 'bout I just come over there now and we'll figure that part out."

"But what—"

The phone goes dead in my ear. I hold it there for a second, trying to get a grip on what's happening to me. The truth is my entire life has changed from something palpable and relatable to something I can't even describe with regular words.

I'm still holding the phone when I hear something moving and look up to see Donnie hovering in the air overtop the kitchen table.

(Frankie)

I try taking a nap but there are sounds in the living room and even though I can sorta convince myself it's just the wind moving the drapes, I can't help picturing Granny in there digging into her little bookcase like a dog, tossing its contents all across the living room floor—which is pretty much what happens every time I leave the house. Today when I got home it was the books all over the floor and all the cabinets opened up in the kitchen. Yesterday the TV came on while I was in the bathroom and I almost had a heart attack going back in there to shut it off.

After a while I get up and make a coffee, but just as I'm pouring the water the phone rings.

"Frankie?" It's my Aunt Annette, who is probably the last person in the world I feel like talking to right now. "How are you?"

"I'm okay," I say, and then something hits me so suddenly and with such clarity that the fear and all my worries get washed away with one simple question. I'm the one who asks it: "A u n t Annette, is Granny there?"

"Is she here? No, of course not," she replies, and right away I know I got a story, a good one—even better than the one I told Ali. It's so simple: Granny wasn't here when I got home this afternoon. I looked around but couldn't find her, so I figured she prob'ly went to somebody's house for the day, or maybe even walked down to the store. I was just thinking she might show up at any minute.

"Does she always walk to the store by herself?" Aunt Annette asks.

"Ahh, not really," I say automatically. It's not 'til after I say it that I realize it's the best thing I coulda possibly said.

Aunt Annette says she'll be over in an hour.

The moment I hang up I do something I been wanting to do since the night I dumped Granny in the landfill: I start tearing through her drawers and closets.

I find money. A lot of it.

There's 140 dollars in the pocket of a raincoat. There's 221 dollars in a box underneath the bed. I know there's more so I keep looking: beneath each drawer in her dresser is an envelope filled with tens and twenties. When I get done with the bedroom I go up into the attic and open up some boxes. There are clothes here, old blankets, lots of pictures, and more money: a small unlocked safety box with fives and tens, all dated before the 1970's. It's hot as hell up here and I'm sweating my ass off but I know there's more—some twenties stuffed into an old shoe, old coins in a box of Gramps' junk, expensive-looking jewelry, more money.

I take the safety box downstairs and shove everything I've found into it before carrying it outside and throwing it into the trunk of my car. By the time I get back inside and straighten out the drawers and the closets (knowing there's still more, there has to be), I hear the sound of a car pulling up into the driveway.

It's no real surprise to find, as I'm walking through the living room to greet Aunt Annette, that the books have been tossed all over the carpet once again.

eight.

(Dale)

I left work around six then ate hamburgers at the diner while trying to figure out whether or not I should drive all the way down the shore. *Maybe I should just go to Mom's*, I was thinking, but she's an hour away in Lansdale and the thought of driving all the way out there to sit and watch my parents watching TV… it's just not the kinda thing you do when you're depressed, unless you wanna get even more depressed.

In the end I decided I'd go down the shore but that I'd stop by Rick's first to see if maybe he might wanna go. I know he doesn't have a show tonight but I also know getting him to go out will be pretty much impossible. But I try it and that's why I'm here right now, standing outside his window, watching something I'm not sure I can even describe right.

What I can say for sure is this: Rick's in there, with another guy. The guy looks sorta familiar, in a weird way, like he's from a book or a movie or something. The thing is, Rick and this guy are not completely on the ground. There might be some kinda wires holding them up but from where I'm at I can't see any.

I turn my head and look up at the sky just to settle my eyes on something solid and regular.

There's a low-flying airplane up there, some stars behind it.

I look in through the window again. Rick is still not really on the ground. The other guy is hovering just above him. They're not dancing, they're not fighting, they're not having sex—it's definitely nothing like that—but even though I'm looking right at them I just don't know what on earth they're doing.

I squint and wave slightly to get Rick's attention; he sorta turns his head but you can tell he's not seeing anything. I'm still waving when I notice the other guy's head turn toward me. Something about his face is strange and blurry, but one thing's for sure: his eyes are orangey-red and they're staring right at me.

I run back to the car and take off, real fast.

At the end of the street, I pull up against the curb and turn the lights off. My heart is beating like crazy because I have never seen anything so messed-up in my life. It feels like I'm hallucinating. Maybe I am. *Am I?*

There's a candy bar in my glove compartment which has melted then re-formed itself several times in the past few days. But right now, it looks alright so I open it up and eat it. It tastes pretty good. You can see Rick's house from the rear-view mirror so I focus on it for a couple minutes but nothing happens. I'm worried that maybe he might need some help, but the thought of going back there gives me the creeps. Maybe it's just some kooky exercise thing Rick's getting into? Whatever it is, it's probably none of my business.

I turn the lights back on and drive away.

ᄃ◯ᄀ

I'm on the Black Horse Pike maybe half an hour later when something happens: the windshield starts rattling and the car feels like it's lifting off the ground but then suddenly I'm not driving anymore, I'm holding my hands out in the air over the steering wheel and screaming because somebody or something is squeezing my head from behind. Later, the car is floating over a supermarket and I'm hugging the door and crying, and then I'm in the backseat singing a Barry Manilow song at the top of my lungs—screaming it, actually—with a guy in a dog suit who is behind the wheel, presumably driving the car. I don't feel tired but as I'm trying to focus on what's beyond the windshield my eyes close and before ya know it, I'm out like a light.

I wake up on the beach in Ocean City, New Jersey. I can tell it's Ocean City because of the Music Pier to my left and the boardwalk behind me. The sun is just coming up and it's windy. For a minute I'm kinda relaxed but when I try to remember how I got here I can't, so I stand up and when I do I see the spot on the ground where I was just lying is soaked through with a big wet puddle of blood.

(Rick)

"How's that feel?" Donnie asks, wordlessly.

He has flipped my body upside-down so I'm facing the ceiling, but at the same time I can see myself from the ceiling looking down at him flipping me. I think this is technically an out-of-body experience, but I never expected something like that would feel so normal. It's just me up here and me down there, no big deal.

Everything turns to white for a second and then we're outside, moving in what might be a small, invisible airplane, gliding over a sea of trees. I blank out for a while but then I wake up behind the wheel of a car that's moving really, really fast. I look back and see Dale Bursmith lying unconscious in the backseat with something very large and very hairy sitting beside him. When I look out through the front window I notice there's no road, and then my vision goes blank again.

Before this, or right after, there is something like the dream I had the other night, or the movie I saw with the people being eaten in the apartment. Except this time, it takes place at a supermarket with several customers in it. If it's a movie, then Donnie's in the lead role, and I guess I'm filming it. The camera is wobbly but it gets steadier during a scene in which Donnie is hanging from a bald guy's shoulders while gnawing on the back of his head. There are other people moving and one of them comes right up into the camera: From where I'm at, I can see a pair of hands that look sort of like mine dig into his face, squeezing at both ends while the thumbs push into his eyes until this milky purple-black shit explodes out of the right one. The camera comes closer and you can see a tongue and taste this warm metallic stuff before the car is moving again, with Dale Bursmith still conked out in the backseat and the smell of the ocean all around.

Later, I'm in the house again. Donnie is asleep on the couch and I'm staring at him. There's a knife in my hand and it looks like I'm thinking about sticking it into his chest. Just when I realize what I'm about to do, I drop the knife and walk upstairs to my bedroom. It feels like I've been asleep for a week and yet the only thing I want right now is more sleep. A song comes to my head the moment I lay down and for the first time in what seems like ages I get the urge to stand up and walk to the studio to record it.

Instead, I start to hum it, hoping it'll still be there, somewhere, when I wake up.

(Frankie)

Aunt Annette used to have curly hair and thick, old-school glasses. She wore loose dresses and oversized shorts and the same cheapo white sneakers for years. Her voice was, and is, high and whiny with a thick South Philly accent. Beyond the voice, though, I almost don't recognize her when she walks into the house.

It's been over a year since I've seen her, and during that time she's totally like revamped her appearance in every possible way: The glasses are gone, she's got short blonde hair (it used to be a mottled-brown), and this air of confidence that gives you the impression she will kick your ass if you look at her funny.

I get a lump in my throat, say, "Hi Aunt Annette," and start repeating my story over and over in my head. You can tell she totally believes the parts I say out loud, which is cool. She doesn't really seem all that worried or upset either, though she does keep looking at her watch and huffing like she's on some kinda tight schedule. Maybe she is?

"So, when was the last time you seen 'er?" she asks.

"I don't know, you got me thinkin' about that," I say, expanding a bit. "I noticed she wasn't here when I got home from work but then again, I don't actually remember seein' 'er last night when I got home or this morning. She coulda left last night, and I just didn't notice. I mean I just assumed she was here sleepin'."

"Uh-huh."

Aunt Annette makes a circular tour of the house, even pulls down the ladder to the attic and climbs up for a cursory look-see. When she gets back down, she asks, "You gonna be here tonight?"

"Yeah, yeah, for sure," I say, and just in case she doesn't realize it, I tell her, "I mean I guess I been pretty much livin' here since Gramps died. I ain't here all the time but I make sure she's got bananas and oatmeal and them candies she likes. I only been tryna help 'er out, ya know? It doesn't seem like anybody else comes around to see 'er much."

"I'm glad you're with her, we all are," she says, though I have no idea who *we all* could possibly be. "It's the only thing that's kept us from puttin' 'er into a home."

It never really struck me that I was actually doing anyone any good by living with Granny. Hearing Aunt Annette say it like that makes my eyes water, and I can literally feel a thick layer of guilt lifting up offa me.

Aunt Annette asks, "So whaddya think we should do?"

"I don't know, either call the cops now or wait 'til like tomorrow? I'm not gonna lie, I'm kinda worried."

"Frankie, she's old, she's not a kid, she mighta just got it into her head to take a bus somewhere. Who knows? If she's not back by tomorrow mornin', gimme a call and we'll go to the police station and fill out a report."

"Maybe you oughta call the cops tonight, just to let 'em know."

"Yeah," she says, but you can tell by the way she says it that she either doesn't want to or doesn't have the time. I'm fine either way: Seeing her has turned out to be a major relief, and I'm gonna feel confident telling my story to the cops or anybody else that needs to hear it.

(Gia)

Despite some *serious* misgivings, I stop at Rick's house after work today.

The place is even worse than I expected.

The door is wide open when I get there and the whole downstairs is wrecked—I mean like totally wrecked. There's records thrown all over the place, the couch is upside down and torn apart, the tables are all knocked over. I'm in shock so it takes me a while to say "Rick?" but when I do it's louder than I meant to say it. There's no response, so I step back outside and walk around the house, looking into each window as I pass it. The back door is open too and the kitchen's just as messed-up: Dishes smashed, the 'frigerator door opened and leaking all over the floor. I walk through into the living room then up the steps, saying Rick's name again, a little quieter this time.

It's not until I get to the toppa the steps that I hear music, an unplugged electric guitar playing a series of notes, then repeating the same thing over and over. I knock on the studio door but nobody answers so I hold my breath a second and push it open.

Rick looks up from his chair and slowly pulls the headphones from his ears. His eyes are lined with black circles and his lips are all dried-up and cracked. There's something all over his shirt and I tell myself it's ketchup or hot chocolate but I know I'm lying. I know what it is.

Rick rubs his forehead and yawns.

"Hey," he says.

"Rick, did'ja get robbed?"

"Did I?"

"Did'ja?"

He shrugs, says, "I don't think so," then stands up. "What's wrong?"

I start backing up, legitimately freaking the fuck out.

"Rick, the whole place is wrecked. You didn't hear anything?"

"I don't know."

"You don't know?"

He shrugs again and it's all I can take. "Oh, man," I say. "I'll be downstairs, okay? We should think about callin' the cops, I think."

"Really?"

I don't say anything else, there's no point. And I'm not calling the police—it's not just because I'm not sure the place was even robbed, it's because I don't want them to see Rick like this. He looks like a maniac.

Downstairs, I pick a yellow-vinyl copy of The Cramps' *A Date with Elvis* off the ground and put it back into its sleeve. It's quiet and gross down here and after a few seconds I can hear the sound of the unplugged guitar playing that same song over and over. It's fuggin' creepy.

This is a much, much bigger problem than I know how to deal with.

I leave the house and I don't look back.

nine.

(Frankie)

Eric lives like ten minutes away in Bellmawr. I can't remember ever asking him for a major favor, but I gotta do it this time—I gotta get ridda the box. As I pull up in front of his house, I pop the trunk and then snap the box open, exposing a pile of bills that makes me feel a little lightheaded. There's no time for counting so I grab a decent chunk of it and shove it deep in my pocket.

Inside Eric's, I hold up the box and say, "You mind if I hide this in your basement or like under your bed? It's not drugs, I swear."

He takes the box from me and shakes it.

"Money?" he asks.

"Yeah."

"Did you steal it?"

"No. I found it." I give him the same story I told Aunt Annette, feeling kinda guilty about lying but then redeeming myself by admitting the tale of the hidden cash. "I got no idea how much is in there."

"Why don't we count it?"

"Alright."

We go up to his room and spread the bills out according to denomination. I'm all wound up so Eric does mosta the counting.

"My Aunt's pretty cool and all but she's like Granny's daughter, right? So if Granny's gone it means my Aunt would get everything, since Gramps is gone and their only other kid was my Dad, and he's dead, too."

"Your Aunt got a lotta money?"

"She's not like a ka-billionaire but they got a big house and a couple nice cars and a lake house too, I think. She's always been nice to me and I don't wanna feel like I'm stealin' from 'er but technically right now this money could pretty much be anybody's, right?"

"You think there's more of it in the house?"

"I don't know," I reply, though I'm absolutely sure there is.

The tally: 2,148 dollars. This is like ten times more money than I ever even seen at one time, and we didn't even count what I got in my pocket.

"Man," I say, "that's fuckin' nuts."

"You know I'd never touch it," Eric says. "You can leave it here with me as long as you want. I think maybe later on you won't feel so bad. Your grandmom liked you before she got sick, she was always tryin' to make you fat. She woulda wanted you to have somethin'."

I stop and think about that for a minute. What would she have wanted me to have? What do I even really want?

"We could make a record," I say, picturing it actually happening. "I mean a *REAL* one, on vinyl, not just a crappy handmade tape. How much do you think that would cost?"

"I dunno."

"We definitely got enough songs to make a record, right?"

"We got enough for like ten albums."

"Think about it," I say. "We put out a record, like independently. Then we use the money we make from that to book some shows. I don't know, Rick Bowen's a weird dude but people like him in Philly and it seems like he likes us. He could help us get some notice, don'tcha think?"

"That would be awesome."

"We gotta do it. We got the money now, right?"

"It probably wouldn't even cost half that much."

We start laughing and punching each other around and I get that same feeling I had when I was talkin' with Ali: *I ain't a nobody.*

Alls I ever needed was a break.

Is this it?

(Dale)

After taking off my bloody jacket and burying it in the sand I walk out over the boardwalk onto the street. I'm at 9th and Ocean and there's no traffic at all so I'm figuring it's maybe 5:30 or 6:00 in the morning. There's a 24-hour diner called The Chatterbox just a few blocks up, so after checking to make sure I still have my wallet—I do—I start walking toward it.

I'm less than a block away when I spot my car, parked right across the street from The Chatterbox. It feels super-coincidental, but even though I can tell there's a memory in my head that makes all this stuff make sense, I can't seem to find it.

The keys are still in my pocket so I open the door and climb in. The windows are all wide open and it smells like a barnyard inside; after starting up the engine to make sure it still works, I roll up the windows and walk across the street into the diner.

The hostess seats me in a corner booth and a waitress pops up right away. I look and feel terrible, so when she says, "Rough night?" I can only grumble out a response. I'm tempted to tell her I just lost six hours of my life somehow but I don't wanna freak anybody out, so I just ask for a coffee and some eggs and toast.

"That's your car across the street?" she asks, pointing toward the window after bringing the coffee.

"The tan one?"

"Yeah."

"Uh-huh—it's mine."

"Last night two women sittin' by the window said they saw somethin' funny goin' on in there."

My heart flutters a little. I pour a creamer into the coffee and ask, "Whaddya mean, funny?"

"Not sure. Geno, the busboy, he could tell you what they said better than me. He might've even seen it. Geno, hey."

Geno is young and tall with a tiny nose and fuzzy blondish hair.

"What's up?" he asks.

"What happened with that car last night, you remember?"

"That's your car?" he asks me.

I tell him, "Uh-huh."

"I don't know what it was exactly but these two women sittin' next to the front desk jumped up alla sudden and one of 'em shouted *"Jesus, look at that!"* and when I turned alls I saw was somethin' movin' away into the street, like? I thought it was a bear or somethin' but then it just like disappeared." He snaps his fingers. "Whoosh, gone."

"Just like that?"

He nods, adds, "The other lady said when the car pulled up there was nobody drivin' it. Then, what it was they screamed about, the window rolled down and somethin' flew out."

"Somethin', you mean like that bear you saw?"

"Prob'ly not really a bear, but somethin' like it."

I take a sippa the coffee.

"Them ladies mighta been drunk," he adds, "but I definitely wasn't."

"Hmm," I reply, and when I look over at the waitress, I notice she's looking at me like she's waiting for me to admit something I did. Like I'm guilty of, I don't know, hurling a bear outta my car?

"I just woke up on the beach," I tell them, defensively. "I don't know how I got there. I don't drink, I'm not crazy. I had a rough day yesterday and I just felt like gettin' away. But to tell you the truth, I feel a little funny myself."

Geno whistles, says, "Yo man, that's nuts," then goes back to work.

"You think maybe you were abducted?" the waitress asks.

"I don't think so," I tell her, "but'cha never know, I guess."

She gives me a sideways look, then winks and walks away.

(Rick)

Uh. I'm having another dream. It's really vivid.

In this one, I'm crawling like a crab along the walls and floors of my house. I'm not in full control of my limbs so as I'm moving, I'm knocking things all over the place and bumping my head and arms on tables and dishes and whatever else is in the way. At the end of the dream I'm upstairs, repeatedly whacking my head against the studio door, which won't open.

When I wake up, I'm lying in the hallway outside the studio. I remember something about Gia, then something else about finding a slice of pizza, which I think I want to eat until I put it in my mouth and have to spit it out. I remember Gia yelling at me but I don't know what for, and this memory makes me feel *horrible*.

At some point, I end up inside the studio, the RECORD button down on the reel-to-reel and a microphone in front of my face. I'm singing the background vocals to a song I have no memory of recording: It's slow and sad and when I realize what it is I'm singing, I have to stop for a moment and fold up on the floor with my hands covering my face.

I'm still on the floor when I hear footsteps coming up the stairs.

"Hey, Rick," comes a voice from the doorway. "How's it going?"

"Donnie," I say. "Donnie, I'm *such* a mess right now."

"No shit?" He lights a cigarette, ignoring the NO SMOKING sign I've got posted on the wall right across from him. "Still feeling good enough to record though, right? I read somewhere you write like three or four songs a day. Is that true?"

I think about this for a moment, and remember that, yeah, it is true—at least it used to be, up until maybe two or three weeks ago. "I haven't been myself lately," I tell him. "I don't know how much I really like what I've been doing."

"So maybe it's time you started doing something new."

It occurs to me suddenly that Donnie has not been a very good influence: whenever he's around, I feel like I'm eight years old, too scared to speak my own mind and not smart enough to comprehend how weak I really am. Other things occur to me as well, particularly the fact that all this awful stuff that's been happening started the night I met Donnie. Since then, I've been losing long stretches of time, dreaming horrible things, treating Gia like shit, and blowing off gigs left and right. The message light on my machine has been blinking like crazy for I don't know how long, yet I can't seem to hit the button to hear who is trying to reach me and why. It feels like I'm disintegrating.

Donnie's face changes while I'm thinking, like he's sensing my thoughts. He sits down on the floor in front of me and runs a hand through his hair, loosens his ponytail then reties it. A flicker of ash falls from his cigarette and lands on his black pants; he whisks the gray smear away with the back of his hand and smiles sideways up at me.

"I realize things have been tough," he says, "but in the end, believe me, this will all be for the best."

"What will?"

"The big change, the big move. You know something's gonna happen and I can *guarantee* you it's gonna be good."

"I don't really feel all that good about anything right now," I say.

"That's because you hit the bottom, which is where you gotta go if you wanna start fresh, for real. Total blank slate, *tabula rasa*, right?" He nods, lights a cigarette from the one he's already smoking. "Life isn't always a fairy-tale, Rick, it gets nasty sometimes and the only way to get through it is to work and work hard. Even more important, *you gotta have a plan.*" He crushes his cigarette out on an old E.L.O. eight-track lying on the floor beside him. "Now here's *our* plan," he says. "We already got a head-start, 'cuz the first step we needed to take was getting you where you are now."

"Where's that?" I ask.

"Rick, you are absolutely nowhere, my friend. You're nothing. That's pretty much how you feel, am I right?"

I nod because it's totally true.

"The next step," Donnie continues, "is to start recording. In fact, I think we're gonna start right now. I'm gonna play the guitar and you're gonna play bass. We're gonna record ten songs and these ten songs are gonna be released on a record by O.L.C. Records. This album's gonna sell like fucking crazy. There's gonna be a single, videos, a tour, and big money." He puffs at his cigarette, leans back. "Rick, what I'm offering you here is something many folks would give their left ass-cheek for: I'm gonna show you how good you can be. Your job right now is to open your eyes and get everything you can outta this, because as soon as we're done, you're on your own."

"What's that mean? Are you leaving?"

"I'm a busy guy—that's why we gotta record this now. The cool thing is, we don't even need to practice. We're gonna get the guitar and bass down in less than an hour and then me and you are gonna go out and fucking kill somebody. And in a couple days, after I'm gone, after you see how freaking awesome you can really be, you're gonna remember how to make your own record."

"What's that supposed to mean? I record all the time."

"You haven't recorded anything like what we're about to record. But this one's not yours—it's mine, 'cuz I put a lotta time into it and it's my idea. Also, I deserve it, and I want it more than you do."

When he smiles, I see something move up his shirt and for an instant there are snakes all over the floor in place of Donnie so it must be a dream, a dream I wake from later with my fingers wrapped around the neck of a bass, looking up at Donnie with my electric guitar in his lap, his head nodding just as the tape in the reel-to-reel runs out and starts to flutter.

ten.

(Dale)

I'm still at the Chatterbox. I'm gonna get fired today if I don't call in sick but I couldn't care less—I hate that job. *Hate it.* I hate wearing a tie and sitting behind a desk, I hate acting like a boss when there's trouble with some dumb customer. I'm a terrible manager, but that's mostly because I don't wanna be a manager.

There's a payphone by the bathroom and I feel like it's talking to me.

I get up and pay my bill and ask for quarters with my change. I'm cringing 'cuz I don't really wanna do this, but I walk back to the payphone with the coins in my hand, ready to either call out sick or tell Ms. Leo I might be a couple minutes late.

When I pick up the receiver, though—even before I drop a quarter into the slot—I can hear the sound of someone breathing on the other end.

"Hello?" I say.

"Hello, Dale," says a voice through the receiver. I bring the phone down to my chest for a second and surveil the room. The restaurant is half-full, mostly with old people yapping and sipping coffee. Nobody's paying any attention to me at all.

I slide the receiver back to my ear.

"Who's this?" I ask.

"I'm a friend of Rick's—I'm actually at his house right now. We were wondering if you might like to stop by and help us with some back-up vocals today, tonight."

I'm looking at the phone because I still can't figure out how this voice got on the line. The phone didn't ring and I didn't call anybody.

"How did you know this was me?"

"Because you're the guy I'm trying to reach."

"Yeah, but—"

"Hey, Dale? Shut up for a second and think about this," the voice tells me. "Think about where you are right now and what you're doing, and then answer this question: do you wanna come to Rick's and do some back-up vocals on a surefire platinum record, or do you wanna be a total nobody going nowhere forever?" There's a brief pause, and I can hear the guy exhaling smoke. "You probably have to go to work, right? Well listen to this, because it's the best offer you're ever gonna get from anybody, ever: if you quit your job today—the one you hate, the one you've been on the verge of getting fired from for fuck knows how long—if you quit that job and come here to record with us instead, I guarantee you all your stupid worries and problems will completely disappear, and from tonight on you'll start living your life with a level of self-awareness, confidence, and independence you've never experienced nor dreamed possible."

"What? How?"

He laughs. "It's kinda like evolution, man. For you, it's the next step. You ready for it?"

"Yeah, but—"

The phone clicks dead in my ear and starts to buzz.

I hang it up then glance around the restaurant again then through the window at my car. Just like the phone a few minutes ago, I can feel the car calling to me. I start walking toward it.

Outside, I unlock the driver's side door but pause before getting in: on the roof there are a series of scratches and smears of what looks like dried blood. A thick patch of fuzz or fur is hanging from the roof rack. In the sky above, the sun is warm and the air is pleasant, but I can already feel the night coming.

I climb into the car and head back to Collingswood.

(Frankie)

In the morning I go to the Police Station with Aunt Annette. We give them a picture of Granny wearing a yellow sweater and fill out a report but the officer there tells us Granny hasn't been missing long enough to really be *Missing* and that maybe we should look around for her first. Aunt Annette keeps checking her watch and when we leave she looks mad because we're gonna have to come back and do this all over again in a day or two.

The only thing I feel is *relieved.*

She drives me back to Granny's house then drives off. I'm thinking of calling Eric to see if he wants to record this afternoon but as I'm walking in the door, the phone starts ringing. I grab it on the fifth ring.

"Hello?"

"Hey. Frankie?"

"Yeah? Who's this?"

The voice on the line tells me he works with Rick Bowen and that he got my number from Rick, which is a little surprising 'cuz I'm not sure I ever gave it to him. He keeps talking, though, and is saying something about a recording session at Rick's that's happening soon.

"We'd like you to lay down some drum tracks," he says. "Maybe do some backing vocals? You're a talented kid and I think this could be a huge step in your career."

I'm not sure how to react but one thing I know for sure: the more this guy talks, the more I feel like I'm gonna conk out, like there's some kinda liquid sleep spilling out through the phone into my face.

I'm trying to tell him I'll get there as soon as I can but I lose track of the phone and get lost leaving the kitchen. Things get blurry then eventually go white.

(O)

It's night when I wake up. I'm in my car driving through what looks like Haddonfield, heading toward Collingswood. The car isn't making any sound and there are no other cars on the road, which seems odd but I'm not sure what time it is either, so maybe it's just like really early in the morning?

I sense some motion from the right and hear a loud *swoosh* passing over the car. It doesn't feel like I'm in control of much here so I let go of the steering wheel to test the theory and as expected, the car makes a right turn on its own then begins slowing down. The lights turn off as the car slides into a vacant spot directly in front of Rick's house.

There's a second *swoosh* from overhead, then a third.

My door opens and I step out of the car, looking up at the house. It's dark except for one room upstairs that's glowing orange-red. The silhouette of someone smoking a cigarette appears behind the curtain there. It waves, holding up something in its left hand. As I'm walking across the lawn toward the front door, I realize what it's holding is a pair of drumsticks.

(O)

Rick opens the door before I even knock. He's got a beard and his face is all ruddy.

"Frankie," he says. His eyes are kinda orange in the middle and when I look into them everything in my head gets mushy.

The next few hours are hard to describe. It feels like gravity's not working right inside the studio; my thoughts and my body feel untethered, like they could float off at any second. Also, I know this will sound weird, but there's some sort of semi-invisible animal in the room that, to a certain extent, is controlling my thoughts.

Every once in a while, I sorta regain my composure; each time I do, I'm holding a pair of drumsticks and banging out a beat with a pair of headphones over my ears. Rick is standing by his reel-to-reel with another set of headphones on, nodding his hairy head to the beat. I do mosta the drums for Bee Plasm, but I'm definitely not a great drummer. What I'm doing right now though is fuckin' nuts: it's fast and loud and the timing is perfect. I can't believe it's me making all that racket, but the closer I listen, the more it feels like I'm the only kid in the world who could do this right now.

Whenever I try to see the animal (or maybe it's a guy in a dog-suit?), the only thing I can see is this red blur. At some point, there's a dream where me and Rick and another guy are floating somewhere and later, in a house I never been in before, there's this movie showing in which an entire family is killed and eaten by a group of flying monsters.

But the thing I remember most about the whole night—the only thing that really comes through with total clarity—is waking up on the floor in Granny's living room, with no idea how I got there, my shirt and hands coated with this sticky red stuff, and my head booming with one screaming thought: *MAN, I GOTTA DO THAT AGAIN…*

(Rick)

I spend the next few nights either going to the movies or dreaming about movies in which entire families are murdered by a pack of wild men or animals. There's one night where I wake up behind the wheel of a New Jersey Transit bus with nobody on it. I get a little scared since I'm pretty sure my regular driver's license doesn't let you drive busses, but I manage to steer this one to the train station in Collingswood. It takes a minute to figure out how to open up the door, but as soon as I get it, I hop out and either run or fly home.

All in all, though, I gotta say I'm feeling better.

It's not until Gia stops by today, however, that I realize how much of a change I've made. She looks a little worried, but I convince her to come up to the studio for a minute to listen to the rough mix of what I'm sure is going to be the album that makes me, for what it's worth, a star. After two songs she reaches out toward the recorder and stops the tape.

"Rick?" she says. "Is that really you?"

"It's me on the lead guitar," I tell her, "but Donnie's doing the rhythm guitar. I'm playing bass too—that's how we laid down the tracks—me on bass and him on guitar. Then I went back and did most of the vocals and the lead guitar and got Frankie to do the drums."

"Rick, it's friggin' awesome." She rewinds to the beginning and hits PLAY again; for the next forty-four minutes and thirty-three seconds, I am listening to something so great and powerful I can hardly believe it's me. No more half-funny lyrics about cars and girls. No more wimpy, ironic guitar lines. This stuff is strong, it's real and it's solid… but it's different, too, like nothing I've ever heard before.

"I'm sorry about the gigs," I tell Gia, since Devilbaby had to cancel a couple shows because of me. "I had to work this out, though."

"I know why now," she says. "Rick, you're gonna release this, right? I mean, you have to."

"Donnie's coming by later to do a final mix with me. It might take us a day or two so I might not be able to answer the phone if you call."

"Nah, I ain't gonna bother ya," she says. "You scared me a little. Shit, I'm still scared. I thought you were, like, losin' your mind or somethin'."

So did I, I think, but the truth of it's pretty clear now: the only thing I've lost is the lame, candy-assed side of my personality that's been mired in mediocrity for far too long. What I found in the process is something I always knew was there. All I needed was a little time with Donnie to get it out.

eleven.

(Frankie)

I have a rough-mix of the songs I did with Rick and I play it for Eric. He's staring at me the whole time the tape is playing, and when it's over, he rewinds the tape and starts it again.

"I can't believe it," he says. "That's Rick Bowen? No fuckin' way."

The tape runs through a third time.

Then a fourth. The fifth time we play it, the tape splits and smoke starts coming out of the machine, but we're both so hyped about what we've heard it doesn't matter. Just hearing it has changed us both: you can feel it.

We're supposed to be recording this afternoon but Eric keeps humming the chorus to one of the songs from the tape over and over and his eyes are all glazed over, like he's stoned or about to have a seizure.

"I got an idea," I say all of a sudden, realizing now that whatever it was that happened in Rick's studio is contagious, and easily spreadable. I can't quite put it into words, except to say:

"Let's make a movie."

We are in Eric's room when the film starts. There's no projector 'cuz it's not really a regular movie, but the idea's kinda the same as it was at Rick's. Eric is reaching for his guitar but is also spinning in a slow 360-degree circle; I'm hovering upside down while popping out the half-burnt tape from Eric's boom-box and inserting a shiny new blank tape.

Eventually I manage to grab the drumsticks and Eric gets the guitar in his hands so we start recording.

Today we sound even better than usual. I mean I'm not saying we're great—we know it's sloppy and pretty much unlistenable, but today it just *feels extra good*, and we get like six songs done before we hear the sound of Eric's mom coming up the steps and knocking on the door.

"Dinner's ready, Eric."

He gets up in a daze and opens the door.

"Oh, hello, Frankie," Eric's mom says. "I thought that was you screaming. Are you hungry?"

"Yeah," I say, even though I'm not.

"I made grilled cheese sandwiches."

"Great!" I say.

At the dinner table, things start to change again. I know it's my fault but I can't help it: Eric's Mom winds up in the upper corner of the kitchen with a pint-glass full of vodka tied to her face. Eric is standing on his head on the table, his shirt hanging over his chin. I swim out toward the living room feeling all blissed-out but I realize then that I'm taking a lot of liberties here so I do my best to bring things back to normal when I get back to the kitchen.

Eric and I come out of it in the middle of washing dishes. I'm drying while Eric's washing. His Mom is sitting at the table with another full glass of vodka, looking a little frazzled. Before I leave, I make a copy of the songs we did today then go downstairs to check on the money box. It's still there and it makes me feel rich. That's a good feeling since I pretty much stopped going to work and I prob'ly don't have a job anymore.

(Dale)

It's hard to tell what happened at Rick's house because I don't actually remember arriving there, though I do have this vague memory of singing into a microphone while my back is being rubbed by somebody or something with really hairy hands. It feels like it happened a long time ago but it was probably only last night or the night before.

I know things are different now and it's gonna take a little time to adjust. The daytimes are rough because I don't wanna do anything but sit in my room and think, though occasionally I get up and roam around the house like a zombie, looking for food or blood or something to hug or pet. Rebecca gives me a hard time whenever she sees me.

"You're not yourself," she says. "You're kinda scaring everybody."

"I'm still just big ol' regular me. Not tryin' to make a scene"

"You sure you even belong here now?"

I have to think about that for a minute because the truth is I definitely know I do not belong here anymore. But where do I belong?

❨O❩

The nights are kind of a mystery as well. It feels like I'm sleeping a lot, but in the morning when I wake up I realize I've pretty much been up all night. I'm usually still fully dressed, shoes and jacket included, and a lotta the time I've got blood all over my face and a funny taste in my mouth. Some mornings, I can vaguely recall being with Rick, visiting some stranger's house. Sometimes Frankie's there, too, and some other guy who looks like he's either melting or covered in red paint.

It's dusk outside now and I'm standing in front of the mirror in my bedroom. I can hear Rebecca downstairs talking above some old Smiths record that I used to like but now hate. There are other voices too so I figure there's a party going on. In the mirror, I see I've lost some weight. My face looks lean and my hair's getting long. I've got a beard, too; I don't know how long I've had it. From certain angles, it looks like there's blood seeping from the middle of my eyeballs.

I lay down to think, and as I'm drifting off to sleep I can feel myself rising, while the stale, sweaty stink of my room is taken over by the sweet scent of the sky, and my eyes open to a view of the trees and houses below, all glimmery and full of meaning and life as I swim through the night toward Rick's house.

(Rick)

I have unplugged the phone and locked all the doors in order to do the mix. Donnie arrived yesterday with some equipment—a digital mixer and recorder, a nice new DAT machine, an effects unit, and some other things I've never seen before and don't know how to use.

"This is gonna take three days," he told me, and right now, in the middle of day number two, we've got about six songs mixed to perfection. We do take a few breaks, of course: Donnie brought a whole bar's worth of beer and alcohol, and although I usually don't drink at all, I've found myself enjoying an occasional dirty martini. We also stop at night for a few hours in order to go see a movie at somebody's house, but as soon as we're back and done washing up, it's right back to the mixing board.

I've been up for at least four days straight.

"We should get Frankie to do the cover," Donnie tells me, and because the time often slips when he's around, I turn my head and see that Frankie is already there with us, a set of colorful markers spread across the desk there and his head leaning over a sheet of drawing paper. Dale is somewhere in the house too. We got him to sing some stuff the other night then made him leave but he keeps coming back.

꘠

At three o'clock in the morning at the end of the third mixing day, Donnie hits STOP on the reel-to-reel and rewinds the tape. We look at each other, a pair of bleary-eyed guys who've just spent seventy-two hours working pretty much non-stop on something that's gonna change our lives entirely.

"Whaddya think?" I ask.

"I'd like to hear it," he says, his hand reaching out once again to the recorder, this time to press PLAY before turning up the output volume.

As an album, it flows. It flows like the mighty Delaware River. It flows and it's strong and it's… addictive. I wanna hear it in my car, I wanna hear it on the radio, I wanna hear it in the supermarket while I'm shopping for stuff to mop up the blood and hair on the walls and floors with. There are ten songs and they're all hits: they bend genres and border on creating their own. They're almost too good to be real but there they are: on the tape, in my head, *for real.*

When the tape ends Donnie slaps me on the back and lights a cigarette.

"Yeah," he says. "That's exactly how I pictured it."

Dale appears out of nowhere so we play the whole thing all the way through for him, then again for all of us because we're still in shock at how well it stays together.

Just before dawn, Donnie gathers up his equipment and the rough tapes as well as the masters the songs were recorded on. I feel a little funny about watching the masters leave the studio, but Donnie turns to me and says, "They're safe with me. Now go to your room and take a nice little nap."

"Could we possibly make a copy of them first?" I ask, sounding— and feeling—a little feeble.

Donnie is standing at the top of the stairs. He tells me: "You're on your own now, Rick. The fuck did I tell you? I said it would end like this. It *will* be good for you, I'll even make sure all your little friends get some nice stuff, too. You okay with that?"

"Sure, but you'll send me a copy of the tapes… right?"

Donnie pouts at me without saying anything and while this is happening, the door of the studio closes on its own, right in my face.

I grab the handle and open it back up but in the split-second it takes me to do this, Donnie is already gone.

twelve.

(Dale)

There's a day when I'm looking out the window from my room and picturing myself bursting through the glass and out into the air, and then the next thing I know I'm in my car and it's packed with all my stuff and I'm turning out of our driveway knowing I'm never coming back. It's dark and quiet and there are no cars on the road so I roll all the windows down and start hurling my things out with a feeling of intense pleasure. I don't need anything, don't want anything.

Things have changed so completely over the past week or so that everything from the past seems like something from a movie—one I watched a long time ago, and didn't like all that much. Back then, I never dreamed things could be this natural. Now, alls I can think of is how much better it's gonna get.

❨O❩

It's nighttime. It's always nighttime now.

I stop at Frankie's but there's nobody there so I decide to go to Rick's. He answers the door looking wired and frantic.

"The tapes are gone," he tells me.

He leads me up to the studio and it's a total wreck: There are beer and vodka bottles and pizza plates all over the floor, and wires and mics and pieces of equipment covering every surface. It's all part of the mess created by a couple weeks of intense recording and mixing, and I'm proud to say I was a part of it: I sang the lead vocals on two songs and back-up on two more. These songs ring and echo all around my head: they're perfect in my memory. They will be hits, played all across the country, and—even if it's just for a couple weeks—at the absolute center of the universal zeitgeist that music is to our culture. You will hear people singing these songs and you will know some, if not all, of the lyrics.

Still, even if none of that happens, it wouldn't make a difference. My memory of the recording sessions is clear, stored forever in the inner-speakers of my mind. Just being a part of all this has completely set me free: it was an opportunity to see and *live* the full extent of my potential, without constraint. I'm never going back to the life I lived before this. *Never.*

Rick isn't seeing it from that angle.

"I got a real bad feeling," he says, his eyes now dimmed to a smoldering gray. "I don't really know Donnie outside of recording this album with him. We never actually signed that contract, even though we kept talking about it. And when he left, he took all the masters and the only copy I had. All he left me was an early rough-mix but when I tried to play it the tape snapped and the cassette-player started smoking." He points to a mess of garbled plastic and tape on the mixing board. "He even took the pictures Frankie drew for the cover."

"Rick, stop," I say, dropping one of my hands on his shoulder. "We did somethin' pretty amazing, don'tcha remember? Doesn't it feel good knowin' you recorded one of the most incredible albums anybody's ever heard?"

"It'll be a huge hit, I know that much," he says. "I can feel that— you can, too, right?"

"Goddamn right I can."

"The problem is…" He stops for a second, rubs his forehead with his fingers. "The thing is, Dale, the tapes are gone. We have no master, no proof it was us that did it."

"So what?" I say, almost shouting it. "Rick, jeez, it was the best you've ever been. You gotta be proud of it, you gotta remember how good it was."

"*Was*," is what he says. "It'll never happen again. Not like that."

"How can that be true? You know how to do it now."

The look on his face is grim. I turn and grab a cracked tambourine up off of a turntable and start banging it against my hip in a steady, shimmery beat. It's the same beat as the last song on the album—one of the ones that I sang—and even though for some reason the lyrics elude me at the moment, I can still hum the rhythm. When I get to the chorus, I look over and see Rick is nodding his head along with the tambourine and staring toward the window. He's humming, too, but he's getting the notes all wrong. *Neither* of us can remember the words.

(Frankie)

There's a day when I pull up in fronta Granny's house to find Aunt Annette's car already in the driveway. Inside the house, I find the backdoor open and Aunt Annette on the porch, her hands on her hips and her eyes all screwed up in confusion.

"Mom?" she says.

I wave a hand and say, "It's Frankie."

"Jesus, I thought it was her," she says. "I coulda swore she was just—"

"…sittin' at the table eatin' oatmeal?" I ask

She nods and sits down on an old swing-chair.

"She throws all the books and magazines outta the rack in the living room," I say. "They were all over the floor when I walked in."

"But I just put 'em all back," she says quietly.

"It's gotta mean something," I say, trying to forget the sight of Granny walkin' half-naked out of the bathroom this morning, or the time, just a few days ago—maybe even yesterday—I woke to find her on the couch, pointing a stubby finger at the television screen, her face fevered and insane without her glasses. "I guess it kinda means she's gone… right? We're just seein' a ghost?"

"Unless she's… no, I guess not. Hidin' somewhere in the house?" She shakes her head. "You're right, that's gotta be it."

"Are you gonna sell it?"

"The house? I think we have to prove she's really gone first. That could take some time."

"Aunt Annette," I say, "I have an idea. You have to promise me to keep it a secret first."

"Is it about Granny?"

"It's about money."

Her eyes light up a little and she gives me a slight nod. It's tempting to tell her about the money I already found, but I hold back, and say, "I've been wantin' to search through the place. The attic, the cellar, all the drawers. We could do it together, I guess I'd feel safer."

"You think she might have some money hidden?"

"I'm not sure, but I wanna look now before we go to the cops again. If they search the house and find anything, they might hold it as evidence or just pocket it and say it was never there." I pause because I can see she's already been looking for it: it's why she's here today, it's why she's got that guilty look hiding under her make-up and the nifty hair-do. "We should do this now. We should put whatever we find together and split it fifty-fifty."

I say this firmly because it's the way it's gotta be. She nods after a few seconds and then, together, we start tearing the place apart.

Two hours later, we have reached a total of 4,428 dollars plus some jewelry that Aunt Annette says is worth well over ten grand.

"I'll put the jewelry in a safety-deposit box," she says. "We'll wait a while, a year, two years." She's so excited it almost makes me wanna laugh. "I won't forget you; you can trust me."

"I wouldn't've been able to look on my own," I tell her. "I don't know how much longer I can even stay here, actually—it's pretty creepy." This isn't really true because the creepiness is kinda growing on me. "I need to get another place to live, like soon."

"Whatever you need, Frankie, I'll help you." She pauses, glancing at the wooden shed just beyond the porch. "Have you…?"

"It's locked," I say. "I don't know where the key would be."

"Can't we just… break the lock?"

I nod. "Okay, yeah, there's a hammer under the sink."

Aunt Annette laughs. I laugh, too, and I'm still laughing when I open the kitchen door to grab that hammer.

thirteen.

(...ten months later...)

(Dale)

There's nothing like being in a band—I've learned that. You can try to make music that everybody likes and hope it sells so you can make a lotta money so you can make more albums that everybody likes, but in the long run you're better off just playing to hear and feel and be part of the music you're making. Other people's opinions just mess up your instincts, and how you naturally feel about the music you make is what matters. Mosta the time you don't even notice it, but as soon as someone gives you their little critique, tells you, "I like this song," or "This song needs work," you lose a little bit of your own connection with it; from then on, it will always hang in the air around you balanced by that second opinion.

Well, that's how it is for me anyway.

No one could have predicted how big Frankie and Eric's band would have gotten over the past few months. It happened so fast it was hard to wrap my head around at first. I'm psyched for them because if anyone can get away with playing for real and natural, it's them. They did their first real show in Philly like four or five months ago and I'm proud to say I was up there on the stage with them, singing in front of a packed house at the Khyber and feeling like I could float away at any second.

I still got that feeling.

It's why I'm leaving Philly and Jersey for good. I'd love to stick around and tour with the band but I've already gotten enough out of it to last a lifetime. What I need to do now is *hear my own voice*, and that voice is telling me to *get the hell outta here*.

I haven't given anyone my new address and I don't intend to. That's partly because I don't have one yet. Two nights ago, I was in Ohio—seemed nice enough. Then it was Michigan—some cool stuff. Tonight, I don't know where I am but I'm hoping to be in San Francisco tomorrow. If that doesn't work, I'll go up to Portland and if that doesn't work, I'll hit Seattle, then Vancouver, then whatever comes next.

I live at night now, and during the day I'm either asleep or nowhere. You wouldn't be able to find me even if you tried.

I'm making movies, too. Some of them are scary, but when they're over I always feel good. These movies are not for everyone. I usually play a kind of monster who breaks into someone's house and kills everybody. It may seem redundant at times but the acting feels natural to me; it's the most alive I've ever felt, and when the filming is done, I drift off into the night. It's thrilling and real and exactly how I've always wanted to feel.

(Rick)

Eric and Frankie's first Bee Plasm album came out of nowhere and took everybody by surprise—and that's an understatement. I can think of other lo-fi-type bands from the 60s and 70s but I've never heard anything that matches the energy of this album. And when I look at the back cover and see PRODUCED BY RICK BOWEN written on it, I know I should be proud, which I am. It was hard work pulling that stuff off of their cheap-ass cassettes, editing and re-mastering everything, then ultimately turning what was in reality a mess of poorly-recorded drivel into a solid, thirty-odd minute release.

But I feel hollow too—more hollow than proud. Maybe that's why I don't know how to react to it: every time I hear "Ice Cream Band," the first single, I reach out to turn it off but my fingers never actually reach the button. I know it's me playing the overdubbed bass. I know the effects I used on the voice, the subtlety I used in keeping the scratchiness there while somehow bringing up the vocals (trebly and low on the master) and stifling the firecracker-like snare. In one sense, I'm tempted to ask: *"How the hell did the world fall for this crap?"* But in another sense—the sense that is well-accustomed to the public's love of vapid, no-brainer pop—I feel as if the ears of the world have made a decisive turn for the better.

That song is number one on the charts this week.

The album has just gone platinum.

It's amazing and incredible and they're already off on an ever-expanding tour, with new dates being added daily.

But I still can't feel genuinely good about it.

Let me just admit it: I'm a little jealous. It's not a feeling I'm familiar with, so I'm a little embarrassed, too.

❨O❩

I don't know anything about Donnie, yet I was able to get ahold of him pretty easily. It took four phone calls—one to a friend in New York and three more to the unlisted O.L.C. Records headquarters number in L.A.—to get him on the line.

"Rick," he'd said. "Love that fuckin' Bee Plasm album."

"Yeah, me, too," I replied. "I never really saw myself as a producer but I guess I always wanted to try it."

"You still recording?" he asked.

"Yeah, I got some new songs."

"I'm sure you do."

The line went quiet for a moment.

"Donnie," I said finally, "You took my masters. I don't even have a copy of the stuff we did."

"What stuff?"

My heart sank. "I was just wondering if you were planning on doing anything with it."

"Funny you should mention that," he said. "I've been working with a band from Boston. They got this awesome new single, but we're holding off on it until the Bee Plasm thing dies down. The album's actually already been released but we've shelved the ads and airplay for another couple weeks. The band's called The Petey State, it's a long story about the name but in the end it doesn't matter. These kids are gonna make millions."

I look directly at the phone, sincerely perplexed.

"Man, what are you talking about?"

He pauses, then tells me: "Look, music is magic, right? I mean it's math, too, and talent and other stuff, but the main thing is the magic. No magic, no music."

"Huh?"

"Problem is, there's no magic in money, and my goal, and the goal of this so-called record label, is to make money. Now, you can question our motives, sure; maybe O.L.C. is a front for some demonic underground uprising, maybe we got a sinister master plan to take over the world… and maybe who gives a shit, right? The point is, I have a way of spotting the talent, but sometimes you have to add a little math to hit max profit."

"Math?"

"Let's just say, sometimes the sound doesn't match the image. In your case, you got all the skills, all the creativity, all the drive. You write the songs, remember? You're a natural-born songwriter. But do you have the looks?"

I shake my head. "Are you trying to say you stole the master tapes because I'm not cute enough?"

"What I'm talking about is marketing, Rick. Making the maximum impact. You match the sound with the image, *BOOM*: maximum impact, maximum profit."

He grunted and I could hear him light a cigarette through the line.

"I'm not asking for the money," I said, feeling desperate. "I only want the masters."

"Look for the new Petey State. Actually, just flip around the dial on your radio in three to four weeks and you probably won't be able to get rid of them. Take care, Rick."

He hung up then. I didn't bother calling back.

❪O❫

We've done several sloppy but excellent shows in Philly and are heading to New York tomorrow night. After that, it's Hartford, then Cambridge, then Burlington and Montreal. Frankie sounds half-decent live; he and Eric have this odd way of not facing the crowd while they're playing, instead opting to stare at the back of the stage, while me (on bass) and Gia (with her stripped-down kit) carry the backbone of each song.

But the audiences are eating it up. The place was packed last night, and every show we've booked is totally sold-out in advance.

Like I said, I'm proud, ever-so-faintly proud.

There's money, too, which is nice. I had enough today to go to Third Street Jazz and Rock and blow 300 bucks on some rare records I never thought I'd be able to afford. I also spotted something on the wall, in the *New Releases* section. The art on the front cover caught my attention right away, and the song titles looked suspiciously familiar. The four guys pictured on the back cover were total strangers, though.

As soon as I got it home, I dropped the record onto the turntable and stared with my mouth open at the speakers for forty-four minutes and thirty-three seconds.

It sounds awesome. Even better than I remember it sounding when we mixed it.

He's going to get away with this because I have no proof. Dale said it didn't matter and took off. I wish I could do the same, but music is my life, and I can't shake the feeling that part of it's been stolen from me.

At night, I go to the movies, alone. Sometimes the movies are playing in abandoned lots where nothing but frogs and insects make up the crowd. Sometimes they're playing in dark forests, or along the beaches of the Jersey Shore. They're not always scary but they can get a little sad sometimes.

Tomorrow night I'll be heading up to New York but another part of me will be hitting the airwaves all across the nation. I wish The Petey State all the best. Someday maybe I'll have a chance to record some songs with them—or for them. Maybe my band could even tour with them.

Or maybe we could all just get together and see a movie.

At this point, it seems like it's really all up to Donnie.

(Gia)

I'm on stage at the Khyber with Tina and Jenn, packin' up the gear after opening for Bee Plasm—I'm playin' drums with them, too, so we're leavin' my kit where it's at. The audience is totally pumped; we seriously just put on a kick-ass show and they're still makin' a lotta noise.

"How we gonna keep this up?" Jenn hollers over the noise to me.

"Are you kiddin'?" I yell back. "We're just hittin' our groove, man!"

It's the truth—it seems like the bigger the crowd, the better we get. And as big as the hype for Bee Plasm is right now, we're buildin' up some serious momentum, too. We're on the cover of next week's *City Paper*, and news that Rick Bowen is producing our first full-length album is already startin' to spread. Part of the deal we made with Frankie and Rick and the record label is that Crank Tops would do the entire east coast tour with them, which is why we're here tonight. Our goal is to go out on our own after that and headline the west coast just after our record is released. We'll see what happens but I feel super positive about it.

I don't need anybody to prop me up, but I do need friends, and it feels like everybody around me right now is hittin' their stride at right about the same time. That can't be a coincidence.

Rick's the only one who seems down, but I get it. He's worked as hard—if not harder—than everybody else. But he trusted a guy he didn't know with his best work and now he's payin' for it. I'm not gonna try and teach him a lesson over it, but I've learned mine: ya gotta trust your friends first, man.

Ya got that?

(Frankie)

It's a big show and we haven't practiced. I keep forgetting the words to the songs, even though I wrote them. They're in my head somewhere but once we're on stage and the music starts, they just sorta disappear. Instead, I open my mouth and start making stuff up; for the most part I'm singing about Rick and Eric, what we did today, and so on. On the rare occasions when I turn around and look at the crowd— this ridiculously massive crowd—I can tell they don't know what I'm talking about anyway.

Maybe it happened too fast, but whatever: it happened. We took a big step, put some money into a well-produced album and it took off pretty much overnight.

The critics hate us and they got every right to. They say we're lo-fi, trash-punk, no-style morons. They say we fuckin' suck, we're a fad that'll be over in a couple weeks. We're talentless goofballs. We don't even know what songs we're supposed to play and we're a total mess on stage.

It's all true and so what? The crowds get bigger every night and it feels insane.

We got grumpy Rick Bowen, our producer, carrying us on bass. We got Gia playing drums, too. We got a contract—not with Donnie, but with Rick and his label, which is off to a good start. They're handling the distribution, they've set up the tour, they put the record out and gave us an agent whose name and face I can't remember. Alls I know is it's not Donnie, and although I can't remember what that dude looks like either, I'm definitely glad he's not around anymore.

(O)

This show's almost over—we're on our second encore now and I have no idea what we're about to play. When the music starts, I look at Eric and he looks back at me and shrugs as his fingers slide down the neck of his guitar. I open my mouth to sing but I've never sung this song before.

I gotta sing about something so I sing about the records I wanna make.

I sing about the view from the top of the marquee.

I sing about Aunt Annette. I tell everybody how we split up the suitcase full of old tens and twenties we found in the shed. I mention how sad she used to be and how great she's doing now. I sing about the cop who was hitting on her when we went to the station to file that missing person report.

I sing about werewolves and horror movies.

About a certain old lady buried at the Kindley Landfill.

The tour was only s'posed to last a couple weeks but I'm pretty sure we can make it last a little longer… maybe a lot longer. I got Donnie's card somewhere, too—just in case I need a little advice. But even if I never talk to him again, I think I can make this work. I mean, hey, if I gotta bite a stranger on the neck once in a while… if I gotta strangle some punks at a convenience store… shit, if I gotta take a chunk outta somebody's side late one night… whatever it takes, there's probably a way to make this tour last forever.

about the author

Stephen St. Francis Decky is a multimedia artist and writer whose work has appeared in a wide array of festivals, collections, and museums, including the New Britain Museum of American Art, the Museum of Fine Arts, Boston, and the Museum of Fine Arts, Nagoya, Japan. As a projection and video designer, he has worked on operas, musicals, and video installations with Mountain Time Arts in Bozeman, MT, IlluminArts Miami, and Beth Morrison Projects, as well as many other arts organizations. Stephen has taught animation, film, and video classes at several schools, including Ithaca College, Tufts University, and Lycoming College, and his films have screened at festivals internationally, including the Camden International Film Festival and the VOID International Animation Film Festival in Copenhagen, Denmark. His fiction has appeared in *Philadelphia Stories*, *Berkeley Fiction Review*, and *Luna Negra*. He is the author of *"Make the Bear Be Nice"* – Frayed Edge Press Street Smart Series, No. 6, and currently lives and works in central New York.

www.ingramcontent.com/pod-product-compliance
Lightning Source LLC
Chambersburg PA
CBHW042030120726
47911CB00025B/441